'If that's your resignation, I accept,' he said in a chilling tone. Verity nodded mutely, too afraid of him to speak. He continued in the same icy tone, 'I do not want you to work a full month's notice. This week while I finalise the Bouvier deal will be quite sufficient for both of us,' he concluded, folding his arms in a gesture of finality. Then he leant back lazily in his chair, his eyes assessing her body with a cold detachment.

'That's fine by me,' snapped Verity. 'The sooner the better.' Saul rose from his chair swiftly, his face dark with anger, his eyes narrowed to diamond chips of ice. He grabbed suddenly at Verity's wrist and she gave a cry of surprise at the crushing strength of his grip. 'I shall expect . . .' He paused, a cruel smile curving his sensuous mouth. 'No, demand,' he added, 'your respect till you leave my employment.' Verity did not reply, but she matched his gaze with equal strength.

'You do need a reference,' he continued, annoyed by her lack of response.

'Yes, Mr Easton,' Verity answered, gritting her teeth.

For the Butterflies

CIRCLES OF DECEIT

BY

CATHERINE O'CONNOR

MILLS & BOON LIMITED
ETON HOUSE   18-24 PARADISE ROAD
RICHMOND   SURREY   TW9 1SR

*First published in Great Britain 1992
by Mills & Boon Limited*

© Catherine O'Connor 1992

*Australian copyright 1992
Philippine copyright 1992
This edition 1992*

ISBN 0 263 77510 0

*Set in Times Roman 10 on 12 pt.
01-9204-53623 C*

Made and printed in Great Britain

CHAPTER ONE

'I WANT five copies before ten a.m.,' he barked, in his usual clipped tone. Verity didn't even bother to raise her head; she was totally indifferent to his abrupt manner. Though she could well understand why he had managed to have four secretaries in as many weeks.

'Did you hear me?' he demanded, his voice taking on a steely edge.

Verity raised her soft sapphire-blue eyes slowly, determined not to be antagonised; she desperately needed this job. She smiled serenely. 'Thank you; ten a.m. sharp,' she replied efficiently, taking the papers from his outstretched hand.

He gave her a curt nod and returned to his office. He walked across the impressive room and stood at the window staring out across the frantic city. A frown of concentration furrowed his usually smooth brow and he ran his hand through his thick mane of dark hair in a familiar gesture of annoyance. 'Damn her!' he cursed loudly, kicking the waste-paper basket. It skidded across the highly polished floor; as it hit the wall its contents scattered.

Verity raised her eyebrows as she heard the thud, and shook her head. That poor waste-paper bin certainly had to bear the brunt of his temper, she mused. Verity sighed; she had been warned by the agency how difficult this post would be. Mr Easton was a perfectionist and since the retirement of his secretary they had been unable to find a suitable replacement. Even the high salary was not incentive enough. Within days each secretary had returned complaining that he was impossible, and refusing to go back. Verity had been confident she would cope—no matter how difficult a taskmaster he was she was determined to succeed.

Now, five tiring weeks later, she was beginning to have some doubts. It was only the thought of Hannah that kept her going. She was all Verity had in the world, and meant everything to her. She twisted the delicate band of gold on her finger in agitation; she had hoped that once she had proved how competent she was his attitude would change. However, he was still as rude and bad-tempered as ever. He certainly lived up to his reputation of being a perfectionist. He had exactingly high standards and expected the same high degree from his secretary.

Verity had never worked so hard in all her life and, though every night she went home exhausted and weary of his constant demands, the following day she awoke eager to face a new challenge. Verity respected him a little more each day despite his abrasive manner. It was hard not to admire a man who pushed himself so hard. Saul certainly was an intense worker; most mornings he arrived before Verity and every night he continued to work after she had left. His business empire consumed him, leaving little time for anything else. He was more like a machine than a man.

Verity enjoyed the hard work—it helped her to forget the past. She worked very hard to impress Saul, as she was determined to gain his respect. If the newspaper stories were to be believed he had little, if any, respect for women. His reputation was legend, but Verity was resolute that he was going to treat her as an equal.

She finished the copies in plenty of time, and rechecked till she was satisfied they were perfect; then she waited. At exactly ten o'clock she rapped smartly on the connecting-office door.

'The report, sir, five copies,' she said quietly, enjoying these small triumphs.

'Put them there; I'll check them later,' he replied dismissively, his head still bent on to his work, the sharp outline of his handsome face softened by the desk-lamp. Verity felt her heart race every time she saw him. He was undeniably a very attractive man. He exuded a sexuality that even penetrated Verity's ice-cold reserve; but she never showed it.

'There's no need; they are perfectly correct,' she retorted quickly. He lifted his head swiftly, his alert eyes narrowed dangerously, a glint of anger apparent.

'I shall check them later,' he repeated, the iciness of his tone sending a chilling shiver down her spine.

'Yes, sir,' replied Verity meekly, dropping her gaze and depising her own weakness, but to lose such a high salary for the sake of pride was a luxury she could not afford. For a moment she thought she saw a brief flicker of a smile, but it was soon replaced by his usual harsh granite features.

He kept his eyes fixed upon her, their icy blueness brilliant and clear. Verity was grateful that she did not blush easily, for his gaze was penetrating and insolent. She returned his stare with equal candour, warm sapphire-blue confronting cold ice-blue. Verity remained resolute under his perceptible examination, betraying none of the turmoil she felt inside. His cold eyes swept over her body with slow deliberation. He carefully appraised her long legs, and though her body was slender it had certainly become more curvaceous since Hannah's birth.

Instinctively Verity self-consciously smoothed down her skirt as she felt the intensity of his gaze upon her. She had hoped to buy some new clothes but, with Hannah just starting school, her daughter's new uniform had taken precedence. She only possessed two smart suits which she constantly interchanged for work; now she felt desperately ashamed under his critical eye.

Verity took a deep, calming breath; she had been doing yoga now for a number of years, and was quite proficient. She had begun while she was at college and found it so relaxing that she had continued. It certainly had given her an inner peace—especially during the fraught time before Hannah's birth. Now she always retained a serenity regardless of how difficult a situation became. However, standing meekly while Mr Saul Easton viewed her so impertinently was becoming increasingly irksome.

'Will that be all, sir?' she asked coolly, determined not to show any emotion, yet her insides were a mass of screaming nerves...

'For now,' he replied, his calculating eyes still fixed upon her. Verity smiled graciously and left his office with as much self-possession as she could muster under his watchful eyes.

She sat down and closed her eyes and began slowly to relax each part of her body, surprised by the amount of tension she felt. He certainly stirred feelings within her that she was determined to deny, yet it was becoming increasingly difficult. It took several slow deep breaths, and finally she regained her tranquillity, but her peace was soon shattered by his harsh voice on the intercom.

'I have some dictation,' he barked.

Verity sighed. He really is an old ogre, she thought as she picked her notepad and several sharpened pencils and went back into his office. He was standing with his back towards her, looking out of the window across the city. She sat down silently on her chair and waited patiently. As he seemed unaware that she had entered, it gave Verity the opportunity to view him with the same clinical observation she had been recently subjected to.

He was an extremely attractive man, tall, powerfully built. He had an athletic physique, lean and hard, and his legs were long and muscular. His dark hair curled softly in jet-black whorls over the collar of his immaculate white shirt. He stood with his legs apart, his hands thrust deep into his trouser pockets. His whole stance was powerful and confident; he exuded an animal masculinity despite his business attire.

Verity felt her blood warm as she looked at him, and her stomach flipped. He turned suddenly and looked with bemusement at her. Aware that she had been caught staring at him, she blushed and immediately tried to become more professional, which was difficult under his curious gaze. She sat bolt upright in her chair, her notepad and pencil at the ready and a look of intelligent expectation on her face. He half raised his eyebrows in mock disbelief then, quite unexpectedly, he smiled. A flashing smile that transformed the whole of his face. Gone was the stern, granite look, to be replaced by a roguish grin, and his eyes lost their chill and shone mischievously.

Verity felt a tinge of pink on her high cheekbones and quite spontaneously smiled back. She felt her blood stir and a dim awakening deep down—sensations that had been denied since that fateful day. She had cocooned herself, not wanting to live without Jonathan. Had it not been for the birth of Hannah, she would have retreated even further into the safe security of a limbo existence. Now, in one brief moment, a sharp ray of light had pierced into her self-inflicted tomb. Her emotions had been stirred and the numbness began to ease.

'Are you ready, sir?' she asked, amazed at the steadiness of her own voice, her eyes dilating slightly as he viewed her with a wry smile...

'Yes,' was his monosyllabic reply, and his countenance changed immediately. He had returned to his usual abrasive self, and it was as if that moment had never happened. It was a full hour later before he finished, and Verity felt elated that she had managed to keep pace with him.

'As soon as possible, Miss Chambers; I want those letters out by tonight,' he instructed her coldly.

'Of course, sir,' she answered as she rose from her chair, feeling annoyed that he did not recognise the amount of effort it took to take dictation at such a rate.

'Take a break first,' he said impatiently.

'Now?' asked Verity in disbelief, her eyes widening.

'Yes, now,' he ordered sternly, his blue eyes glittering, his tone authoritative. He ran his fingers through his hair agitatedly as he looked at her.

'Well, thank you, sir,' smiled Verity, delighted now that he had shown a more human understanding of her work.

'It's for my benefit; I want those letters in tonight's post and I want them correct,' he barked, shattering any illusions that he was showing concern for her.

'They will be ready, I can assure you,' answered Verity coolly, marvelling at her composure and mentally congratulating herself on her self-control. He certainly needs his good looks, she mused silently, as his character leaves a lot to be desired. The man certainly lived up to his terrible reputation.

Stories about his lifestyle were abundant. The few facts Verity knew were patchy, but all were unpleasant. The man was obviously a scoundrel. Some years ago he had eloped with Amanda Ellis, his employer's daughter. Before the year was out he had left her; there was talk of a child but no one was certain. He'd then had a string of beautiful women, and still did, but at the first mention of marriage they were dropped.

Saul Easton was ruthless and determined, and when Mr Ellis signed over the company to him and then retired into obscurity it was rumoured that Saul had forced him into doing so. As a business opponent he was formidable. He was quick to spot a company's weakness and always made his bids at the right time, and over the years Ellis and Easton Enterprises had grown considerably as a result of his astute business acumen.

It was difficult to like a man of such questionable character, so naturally Verity distrusted him. She did not like him but she was willing to tolerate his bad temper, ignore the rumours and even, as his secretary, protect him from any unwanted attention. She did all this with efficiency and serenity, never outwardly reacting to him; though often she felt close to losing her temper, she refrained.

This galled Saul; he had always drawn the attention of females, from nursery onwards—why was she so different? He had noticed the wedding-band but instinctively knew that it was not that which made her so impervious to him. It rankled his ego and he was determined to make her show some emotion. He looked at her disdainfully, his dark eyebrows drawn together.

'Miss Chambers, I'd like a coffee too,' he said, his voice breaking into her thoughts. Verity stiffened immediately; she was always conscious that she was sensitive to him and could not afford to be so.

'Of course,' she smiled, almost too sweetly, which irritated him all the more. He scowled at her as she left his office but she ignored his dark look.

'Coffee, two sugars, a little milk,' said Verity as she offered him his steaming cup of coffee from her beautifully manicured hand.

'Aren't you going to advise me to cut down on sugar?' he asked in a bored tone, as if he had been given the advice many times. He looked intently at her as he spoke.

'It is of no interest to me how many sugars you have, and I doubt you would take any notice of my opinion if I offered it,' she replied, matching his tone and shrugging her slim shoulders casually.

'Aren't you interested in my well-being?' he asked, irked by her lack of concern yet wondering why the opinion of his secretary should be of any importance.

'If it affected my salary, then I suppose it would be of interest,' she answered honestly, her bright blue eyes wide with innocence.

'Is that all I am to you—a supplier of wages?' he stormed suddenly, banging down his coffee-cup and splashing coffee into his saucer.

'What else should an employer be to his employee?' she asked, puzzled by what he had said, though she was used to his sudden outbursts.

For a moment neither one of them spoke, as the tension welled up between them. Their eyes met in a silent combat; momentarily they were locked in an unspoken battle of wills. Verity suddenly thought it seemed a cruel thing to say, and yet it was the truth—wasn't it?

'I'm sorry; that was rude,' she apologised falteringly as she was aware of the compelling intensity of his gaze.

'I have no need of your apology; I prefer a secretary like yourself. Miss Austin was exactly the same; maybe in time you will be of equal value to me. His voice was unemotional though his dark eyes flashed with irritation. Then he turned in his chair to look out of the window, and Verity knew she had been dismissed.

The arrogant swine! she stormed, tranquillity and deep breathing forgotten. I'm like Miss Austin... She was sixty-three, a spinster, plain as a back door, the tongue of a viper, and possessively jealous of Saul Easton. Verity shuddered, as the vision of herself in thirty-eight years swept before her eyes. She shook her head sadly; there was an element of truth in what he'd said—and her life could have been so different.

Verity's eyes grew soft with the memory of the girl she used to be. It all seemed a lifetime ago now. She had grown up a lot since then. She had met Jonathan at art college, fallen madly and passionately in love. The two brief years they'd spent together were perfect, Verity had never been so happy in all her life. They had planned on setting up their own advertising agency. Jonathan would be the creative artist and Verity, because of her patience and attention to detail, would be the finished artist.

Verity shuddered as the unhappy memories came flooding back. Tragically, halfway through their second year at college, Jonathan was killed in an accident. Verity recalled how devastated she had been. She'd suffered deeply, neglected herself and her studies. It was the shock realisation that she was pregnant that had snapped her out of her misery. Now she had something to live for; a part of Jonathan was still alive. Naturally her parents were shocked; they had been so proud of their daughter—the first member of the family to achieve higher education. Now their dreams had been shattered, and the shame attached to an unmarried mother was still embarrassing to them, so Verity wore the old band of gold to protect her parents from gossip.

Yet, once over the initial shock, they rallied round. They had liked Jonathan very much and the thought of a baby was certainly helping Verity cope with his death. It was decided that a career in art was rather futile now, so Verity left college and began secretarial classes and language classes.

After the birth of Hannah, her parents had looked after their granddaughter as indulgently as all grandparents did, and Verity had concentrated on getting as much secretarial experience as she could.

Now she was established as a bilingual secretary the agency could always find her a suitable post, normally paying well above the normal rate. It was just as well, because Verity's parents had left England only last month to begin a new life in Australia. They had both retired, and Verity's brother had been asking them for a number of years to join him and his wife, but they didn't want to leave Verity and Hannah. This time, though, Verity had insisted, as Hannah was starting school in September. It would be easy enough to find someone suitable to look after Hannah for a couple of hours till Verity finished work. In fact Verity had been more than lucky; the small tatty flat she rented was across the hall from a retired nurse, Mrs Collins, who was still very sprightly for her age, and adored children. She soon became firm friends with Verity and a very special aunt to Hannah.

Verity found it hard to imagine any other life than the one she was leading. Though it was a struggle, she was determined to give Hannah as much as she could. The dismal flat was only temporary till she had saved a deposit to buy a house. Verity smiled at the idea of a little house, a neat garden where she and Hannah would sit in the sun. Sometimes she tried to imagine a man there. A father for Hannah; since starting school the little girl had become preoccupied with the idea of a father, and it hurt Verity to think it was something she would never be able to give her. Verity knew she could never love another man; Jonathan had been her ideal—no one could ever replace him.

'Excuse me,' purred a voice, 'is Saul in?'

Verity was jolted out of her personal thoughts with a start.

'Mr Saul Easton—is he in?' the woman purred again, talking slowly as if she were speaking to an idiot.

'Er—yes, I'll ring through,' replied Verity, looking at the arresting woman with a tinge of envy. She was tall, very tall, slim and stylish. Fine blonde hair framed a beautiful made-up face and a pair of sultry eyes stared out at Verity with a look of pity mixed with contempt.

'I'm sure that won't be necessary,' she smiled, revealing perfect teeth; then she walked past Verity as if dismissing a servant and swept into Saul's office leaving a trail of expensive perfume in the air.

'Imogen, how marvellous!' were the last words Verity heard before the door clicked shut on the office. Verity frowned as she sat down and pounded away at her typewriter at a furious rate. Periodically she would hear shrill laughter mixed with the deeper huskier growl of Saul, and she would pound away with renewed vigour. Finally the office door swung open and the tall figure of Saul strolled out with Imogen draped round his arm. She looked as smug as a cat who had eaten the cream, thought Verity spitefully.

'I'm going now; cancel this evening's appointments— I'll be busy,' he said drily, his cold eyes casting a quick look at Verity.

'Of course, sir,' nodded Verity, 'and these letters— will you sign them now?' she asked, offering him the pile of letters with her outstretched hand.

'No, they're not that important,' he replied, shaking his head vaguely.

'Not that important? Well, they were before; you insisted,' snapped back Verity, her eyes bright with anger. She was so annoyed that all her hard work had been to no avail. He frowned, and darted a warning glance at Verity that silenced her immediately. The flash of light in his eyes was as cold as steel.

'I have other priorities now, thank you, Miss Chambers.' She glared at Saul as he spoke, her blue eyes shining with a fiery glint. How she hated this man and the idiot he was with. They stand so close you would think they were glued together, she thought disapprov-

ingly as she awaited his reply. Saul remained silent as if
carefully wording his reply, his teeth gleamed as he broke
into quiet laughter, then he said, 'You're so efficient.'

Verity bristled; her face was set starkly, her mouth a
thin line as Imogen smirked deviously. It was obvious
that whatever Saul had said about her it was not that
she was efficient. Verity felt a bubbling anger growing
inside her, and she stared hard at Saul with a withering
look.

'I knew you would be here. Work is your life, isn't
it?' Saul said smugly, still pleased he had been proven
right. He fixed his sharp ice-blue eyes on her, awaiting
her reaction; his perceptive gaze missed nothing, so her
anger, though controlled, was evident to him.

'Unfortunately, I have to agree, I haven't the income
that allows me the luxury of not working,' replied Verity
coldly, staring at Imogen deliberately as she spoke.

'Well, I'm here to relieve you of your duties; you may
go now.' Saul grinned, aware of the gibe at Imogen. His
eyes swept over Verity's body as if he was comparing
the two of them.

'Thank you,' answered Verity frostily, picking up her
handbag immediately and pulling her old grey mac from
the hanger.

'Goodnight Miss Chambers,' called Saul as she
reached the door; his voice was mocking yet she knew
he still expected a reply.

'Goodnight, sir, goodnight...' She paused, realising
that she only knew the woman's first name, but the pause
was soon filled.

'Don't worry—we will have a good night,' Imogen
giggled again, and moved even closer to Saul, who
wrapped his arm around her. Verity nodded and gave

her a false smile by way of reply. She really did detest that type of woman, who used her very obvious charms so deliberately. She really was a mockery to her sex, thought Verity. She was obviously unable to do anything but spend money and indulge herself. But Verity didn't waste time thinking about her, as she realised that for the first time she would be able to pick up Hannah from school. It made her feel really happy walking up the school drive with all the other parents. She loved Hannah so much that it hurt to be away from her, yet she had no option. At the top of the drive she met Mrs Collins already patiently waiting.

'Hello—not lost your job have you?' she laughed good-naturedly. She was a plump lady with softly greying hair and an easy-going nature.

'No, I've just finished early and I thought I'd come here; it's a privilege I can't often have,' replied Verity, so delighted to be there when Hannah came out of school.

'Mummy, Mummy!' yelled Hannah as she raced out of the school. Verity swept her up into her arms and showered the little girl with an abundance of kisses. She hugged her tightly before putting her back on the ground, then she clasped her hand firmly.

'Hello, darling; have you enjoyed school today?' asked Verity, trying to suppress the anxiety in her own voice. Hannah had not settled well at school, and each morning was a battle of strengths. Verity found it difficult to send her reluctant child to school, but knew she had to.

'No, I don't like school—it stinks,' answered Hannah, screwing up her nose in distaste. Verity laughed at her expression.

'Well, I'm sure you will like it soon,' she reassured her, mentally saying a prayer that it *would* happen soon. Hannah was suitably comforted, and the three of them walked home together. Hannah chattered on happily.

'I'm so glad you were outside; I saw you and told Miss.'

'I finished work early today; that's why I'm here,' explained Verity, clutching her daughter's hand in hers. Hannah's face crumpled as she thought about this and realised her mother wasn't going to be there every day. 'I can't be there every day, but Mrs Collins will always be there; now cheer up,' said Verity, trying to jolly Hannah along; but she felt a stab of sorrow herself, and terribly guilty. Was it school or her working full-time that bothered Hannah so much? she mused silently.

'I know; as it's a special day, let's go to the Pizza Palace and take a pizza home with us,' persuaded Verity anxiously, trying to make amends.

'Let me, Mummy; you go home and set the table. I'll choose the pizza—I'm a big girl now.'

'All right,' laughed Verity, and hugged her daughter affectionately, knowing full well what the pizza would be, but delighted that Hannah had returned to her normal happy self. Mrs Collins and Hannah made their way into the town centre and Verity hurried home; with a bit of luck she would be able to have a bath before they returned.

Verity shivered as she entered the flat; it was cold and damp, the wallpaper was stained with mould and beginning to peel away from the wall. She lit the gas fire and put the side-lamp on; they helped make the room look warmer. Then she ran herself a bath, though she didn't linger; as a working mother she never had the time to soak lazily. Giving herself a brisk rub with her towel, Verity then released her thick dark hair from the taut double plait she wore it in for work. She shook her head as her hair fell luxuriantly around her shoulders, then took up the hairbrush and brushed her hair furiously till it shone. It was beautiful hair, rarely seen at its best, as Verity insisted on wearing it in a severe style for work. She wanted to be appreciated for her skills not her looks.

Verity paused before pulling on her loose tracksuit. She stared confidently into the full-length mirror and was pleased at the reflection. She was tall, slim but there was a definite feminine curve to her body, her legs were shapely and her dark hair framed a strong face. Her almond-shaped eyes were vivid blue, dark yet bright, and long sooty lashes enhanced their eastern-looking beauty. How dared Saul Easton suggest she was like Miss Austin? Verity thought indignantly; then she laughed. The reflection in the mirror bore no resemblance to the prim executive image Verity had at work. If only he could see me now, she thought as the doorbell rang.

'I'm coming, but I haven't made the salad yet,' called Verity as she hurried to answer the door.

'Nor will you be able to without this,' Saul said as he leaned indolently against the framework of the door, proffering a plastic bag of groceries, a lazy smile on his arrogant face.

'Th-Thank you,' stammered Verity, amazed that her secret thought had suddenly appeared. She coloured slightly under his perceptive scruntiy.

'In your eagerness to leave you left these behind; I thought you might need them. By morning the heat in the office would have spoilt them completely,' he stated as his eyes swept over her body with discernment, his face registering surprise, momentarily.

'Thank you; that's very kind of you,' repeated Verity, her heart racing because she was unsure about such consideration. She pushed her loose hair from her freshly washed face self-consciously, and tried to avoid his gaze.

'I'm afraid I don't deserve your thanks—I have an ulterior motive; the report on the Bouvier Company—I have several more new pages that need translating. By tomorrow,' he added sharply, a devilish delight flashing momentarily in his ebony eyes.

'But the meeting is a fortnight away,' protested Verity, angry that she had imagined his visit was for her benefit. She mentally scolded herself. She was his employee, nothing more—not that she would want anything to do with a man with *his* reputation.

'Next week; so you see it is essential,' he explained. There even seemed to be a note of apology in his voice.

'Yes, I suppose so,' agreed Verity, disappointed that she would have to work tonight. Somehow finishing work early and collecting Hannah had put her in a holiday mood. It had been some years since her last holiday, and Verity thrived in the sunshine...

'Shall we go in, and I'll just run through what I want?' he said, walking straight past with his usual self-confidence. Verity was stunned. It was hopeless, she thought frantically; what was she to do now? She tried to think but her mind was in a turmoil and his very presence had made her nervous. Her heart thudded uncomfortably against her chest as she attempted to regain her composure. Any moment now Hannah would return and he would know the awful truth. It was well known that Saul Easton did not employ mothers; he considered them too unreliable. The agency had told Verity to keep her daughter a secret and she had willingly gone along with the deception in order to secure the post. If the deception came out now Verity could well lose her job.

'Please sit down,' said Verity as she followed him in; he gave a nod and sat down on the threadbare sofa. He swept his hand carelessly on the arm of the sofa, disdainfully brushing away biscuit crumbs left by Hannah. Verity gave him a weak smile; his very size dwarfed the already small room and his immaculate clothing shone out against the shabby surroundings.

Verity noticed how quickly he had assessed the room, his distaste apparent from his expression. Most of the furniture was her parents'. It was old but solid and reliable, as they were. Verity had promised herself that once she had enough money she would send them away to a french-polisher's to be restored to their former glory. Saul viewed the whole room in dismay; Hannah had emptied her toy-box on the floor, scattering jigsaws, blocks, dolls and numerous books all over. Verity was annoyed that Hannah had not put her toys away; she certainly was becoming difficult since she had started school, and Verity found herself having to tell Hannah to do things over and over again.

'Do you want a coffee?' offered Verity, trying to gain control in her own territory, and desperately failing. She was suddenly aware of how cold the room was, and shivered. The gas fire, though fully on, made a feeble attempt at heating the damp room—it failed miserably.

'Thank you,' he said curtly, his jaw set in uncompromising hardness as he bent down and idly picked up one of Hannah's dolls. His long, tapering fingers stroked the doll's hair gently and he looked intently at it, a pensive, almost wistful look on his face. Verity watched him with interest, but he was so absorbed in his own thoughts that he was unaware of her presence.

'We're back! Hurry up, open the door!' yelled Hannah excitedly as she banged on the door.

'Coming,' called Verity as she went to the door, wondering how to explain to Saul about Hannah.

'At last; I got extra salami and olives,' said Hannah eagerly as she pushed her way past Verity and rushed on into the lounge. She stopped abruptly at seeing Saul and stared at him in amazement, her blue eyes widening.

CHAPTER TWO

'HELLO,' said Saul, regarding Hannah with equal amazement and dropping her doll on the floor as he stared at her.

'Hello; do you like pizza?' offered Hannah, thrusting the large box into his hands with sudden confidence.

'I'm quite sure that Mr E——' began Verity, but she was interrupted by Saul himself saying,

'Only with extra salami and olives.' He smiled, his whole countenance changing. The cynical expression he usually wore was gone and replaced by a genuine warm and happy smile.

'That's just the one I've got 'cause me and Mummy love them,' Hannah informed him, pleased that he agreed with her choice.

'You set the table, then, and I'll toss the salad,' said Saul as he turned towards Verity. 'Kitchen through here?' he asked, nodding his head in the right direction.

'Er—yes,' stammered Verity, who was unable to believe what was happening. 'But I'll do it.'

'I'm quite capable of tossing a salad.' The sharp edge was back in his voice and his powerful body stiffened as he spoke. He did not wait for Verity's approval; ignoring her completely, he disappeared through the archway into the tiny kitchen. I bet the pots are dirty, thought Verity anxiously as she tried to remember whether or not she had washed the breakfast dishes that morning.

24

'I'll be off,' whispered Mrs Collins conspiratorially, winking at Verity.

'No, no,' insisted Verity. 'He's my boss; he's called round with some work he wants me to do,' she tried to explain desperately.

'Aye, well, that may well be,' replied Mrs Collins smugly, and she nodded knowingly and left. Verity sighed; she would explain to her again tomorrow, she thought, but now she must see to Hannah. She really was a chatterbox, thought Verity, secretly proud that her young daughter could speak so well. Goodness knew what she would be telling him. Verity froze as her worst fears were confirmed.

'Yes, honestly, he is a ogre, isn't he, Mummy?' asked Hannah, her small face deadly serious.

'Who's an ogre?' replied Verity, smiling down upon the upturned face of her daughter and mentally praying.

'The man you work for—he's an old ogre,' laughed a delighted Hannah. 'You're always saying so,' she added, to lend more weight to her argument.

'Is he really that old and awful?' asked Saul, a wry smile playing on his lips, but his eyes were dark and forbidding.

'I'm sorry,' began Verity, blushing red to the roots of her hair.

'It's not the ogre I object to—merely the old.' His eyes were fixed upon her, their ice-cold brilliance piercing into her very being, and Verity panicked as she felt once again a tremor of forgotten feelings. She breathed to steady herself as she met his gaze with equal candour. She sensed there was an anger there—was it hurt pride?—his male ego dented.

He was an extremely attractive man despite, or maybe because of, his super-cool arrogance. Yet perhaps he was not as old as she had previously imagined. He certainly appeared far less daunting perched on a breakfast-stool biting large pieces of pizza than he did in the sombre surroundings of the office. It was the greying hair that edged around his temples that gave him an older, more distinguished look. Maybe he has them tinted in to give the illusion of age; it certainly would be advantageous in the business world, thought Verity as she tried to concentrate on eating her meal. Then she dismissed the thought; he had many faults, she knew, but vanity certainly wasn't one of them.

Throughout the meal Verity was aware of him watching her. She was uncomfortable under his perceptive scrutiny, and felt flustered, so she was grateful that Hannah kept a stream of conversation going throughout. The little girl had taken an instant liking to Saul and he seemed equally delighted with her company, and totally at ease. Verity felt a stab of pain; she had never shared Hannah with anyone like this outside her own family.

'Hannah, I have some work to do; will you please go to play at Mrs Collins's?' said Verity once the tea things had been cleared away. 'I'm sorry, but I have some work to do.' She smiled hopefully at Hannah.

'No, I won't!' Hannah shouted rudely, screwing up her tiny face. She was enjoying Saul's company, and flirting outrageously as did all little girls.

'That's very rude of you; apologise to your mother at once, then do as you're told,' scolded Saul in one of his iciest tones. This startled Hannah, and Verity immediately expected a terrible tantrum.

'Sorry,' said Hannah sulkily, her head lowered and her face set in a scowl.

'You don't sound it.' Saul's voice sounded even icier and he moved purposefully closer to Hannah, his masculine figure dwarfing hers completely.

'I am!' cried Hannah, running over to Verity and wrapping her arms tightly around her leg, frightened by Saul's threatening presence.

'There, there; it's all right. Mummy knows you're a good girl,' replied Verity as she bent down and hugged her little daughter. She glared at Saul as she comforted the distraught child, hugging her fiercely to exclude him; but he merely shrugged his shoulders and looked disapprovingly at Verity's reaction.

'Now off you go and I'll come for you at bathtime. Take an apple and go,' reassured Verity as Hannah skipped away, recovering once she had been rewarded. She gave a gleeful smile of triumph as she passed Saul. He returned it with a cold, hard stare and Hannah faltered for a second before rushing away. The silence that followed was electric. Verity stared at Saul, the contempt evident in her eyes. She was furious with him and a burning anger was growing inside her. Once the door had closed Saul's icy-blue eyes turned on Verity and he spoke, softly, but with conviction.

'You should beware of giving in to her too much; it's not good for her or you.'

'Thank you for your concern, but it really is none of your business,' retorted Verity icily, her eyes ablaze with rage at his arrogance.

'Then I'll show you the work I require, then go,' he answered abruptly, his eyes darkening with fury at Verity's put-down.

'Yes, I think that would be best,' agreed Verity, trying to control her temper and immediately becoming his efficient secretary. She hid her own feelings of outrage at his interference with difficulty. They began to review the documents he had brought, and the atmosphere was filled with tension as they both struggled with their own anger. The work was complicated and detailed and they both had to concentrate on the job at hand. Finally Saul broke the tense atmosphere.

'It is not usually my policy to employ mothers,' he stated, his head still lowered on his work, his thick dark hair falling on to his forehead and into his eyes.

'I fail to see why,' replied Verity, darting a quick glance at his hard, handsome face, aware of his fiery temper.

'I find mothers unreliable; their children always take precedence.' His head shot up as he spoke and he pushed his hair from his face impatiently. His cool eyes fixed on her, causing a rush of colour to her cheeks; her heartbeat increased as she remembered her deception.

'I have an excellent child-minder; she is more than capable of coping,' retorted Verity, trying to remain calm but disliking his high-handed attitude.

'A real hard-headed career woman, are we?' he asked, a trace of anger in his voice.

'Women do have equal rights; I fail to see why I cannot pursue a career and be a mother,' she replied honestly, with an edge of irritation in her voice.

'I prefer to employ women who do not have the distraction of children,' he said sharply, unused to having his authority questioned; yet there seemed to be a smile playing on his mouth, as if he was amused by her audacity...

'Do you wish to terminate my employment?' Verity asked suddenly. She regretted the words once they were spoken; what on earth would she do if he accepted her offer? she thought.

'When and if I decide to review your contract it will be as a result of your failing to fulfil my requirements. At the moment you are...' he paused '...satisfactory,' he concluded grimly.

Verity was furious. She had never met such an arrogant, self-opinionated man in all her life. How dared he describe her work as 'satisfactory'. He was unable to comprehend a word of this document. His command of the French language consisted of a menu! she thought angrily. She fumed inwardly but remained completely serene towards him, forcing herself to smile.

'I'm glad that you find my work acceptable; I shall endeavour to retain the same standard, and the fact of my being a mother will not interfere with my work.' She spoke with a cool efficiency she was not feeling. She knew it was a lie; Hannah would always come first.

'Good,' Saul replied curtly. 'I hope you will have this work prepared for morning,' he said as he rose to leave. Verity nodded in response. He began to put on his coat and Verity suddenly felt lonely. It had been nice to have a meal with another adult. Once Hannah was in bed, the nights were long and boring; at least tonight she would have some work to do, she mused, trying to make the best of it.

'I'll nip out for Hannah; I think she would like to say goodbye.'

Saul raised his eyebrows in an expression of doubt, and Verity could not help but smile. She disappeared, returning within moments with a boisterous Hannah.

'I'm back!' shouted Hannah as she burst into the room.

'So I see, or rather hear,' smiled Saul indulgently as she hurried in.

'Say goodnight to Mr Easton, then pick up your toys while I run you a lovely hot bubbly bath,' said Verity kindly, her eyes full of all the love she felt for her daughter.

'I'm far too tired, Mummy; you do it and I'll go and take my clothes off,' answered Hannah as she skipped out of the room. Verity sighed and shook her head; she half-heartedly picked up the toys and began to toss them into the large cardboard box that was used as a toy-box. Saul watched with a frown; his dark eyes followed her every move, but Verity was too busy to notice.

'You spoil her; she needs a firmer hand.' He looked intently at her as he spoke, his eagle-sharp eyes noting her reaction. Verity was already angry at his previous interference; even her parents, who for a long time had taken a great deal of responsibility for Hannah, had never intervened. Yet this man hadn't been in her home for five minutes without proffering his opinion. She stiffened and turned to look at him; their eyes met. She wanted to look away but he compelled her attention.

'I understand you are not married; does the father take no interest in her well-being?' he demanded roughly, a cutting edge to his voice. Verity's anger registered immediately; it was painful enough having lost the man she loved, but for someone to suggest he wouldn't care was too awful for words. She glared at Saul with barely concealed contempt.

'How dare you?' she spat, her blue eyes blazing with the increasing anger she was feeling. 'He would have done anything for me and her.'

'Except marry you—or was he already married?' interjected Saul grimly. That was too much; regardless of the consequences Verity reacted quickly. Jonathan had been everything Saul Easton was not—kind, generous, with a happy disposition and a wonderful sense of humour. Verity stared with horror at the reddening mark on the side of his face; she had felt her hand strike him, had seen his head recoil as the full impact struck him, and yet all she truly remembered was her own voice screaming, 'Shut up! Shut up!'

She stared at him, her eyes wide with disbelief. Suddenly she was aware that she was totally alone with a man renowned for his temper. He towered above her; his jaw had hardened and a dangerous light flickered in his eyes. Verity sank into the chair, her heart racing against her chest. She was weakened by her own emotional outburst. He remained motionless, watching her closely with ice-cold eyes. She could see a pulse beating strongly above his greying temples. His eyes momentarily widened, then they narrowed to granite chips. He clenched his fist till his knuckles were white, the movement running up the tendons in his arm. The atmosphere was so full of tension that it was at breaking-point.

Verity held her breath; his icy gaze made her fearful. She could feel her heart thudding violently against her chest and instinctively she placed her hand at her heart, almost willing it to slow down. He moved suddenly and Verity shrank back and closed her eyes tightly, almost as if she expected some retaliation. She heard the door of her flat slam loudly and breathed a sigh of relief. Then, as the full horror of what had just taken place and the inevitable consequences struck her, Verity lowered her head and began to cry.

She didn't sleep well that night; she tossed and turned repeatedly, trying to settle, but it was hopeless. By the morning she was weary and she trudged to work miserably. The thought of facing Saul weighed heavily on her mind. She felt sick; though she desperately wanted to be strong there was a nagging fear in the pit of her stomach. He was a difficult man to work for but to slap his face... Verity shut her eyes and shuddered at the memory. It was so unlike her to react that way. She was still angry with him, yet she felt more anger at herself. She had over-reacted. She knew deep down that it had not been just to protect the memory of Jonathan. She had slapped Saul because he had angered her; many times he'd aroused feelings in her he had no right to, and this was the last straw. He had pierced through the vacuum she had put herself in, and Verity hated him for that. He seemed to have the ability to niggle her. He had, with slow deliberation over the last month, made small inroads into her feelings. It was only now that Verity was beginning to feel the cracks in the armour-plating that she had moulded around herself, determined never to feel again. Now it was beginning to weaken, and that frightened her.

Verity sighed; it was painful to wake up emotions after so long. She felt she had betrayed herself in revealing an emotion—even if it was only temper. Now, because of her outburst, she could lose her job. It was pointless to dwell on it, Verity thought soberly; she must just remember to keep calmer next time. She glanced around the office with relief; at least he didn't appear to have arrived yet.

She went into the office and sat down, trying in vain to work out exactly what she would say, though the thought of an apology stuck in her throat. She knew she would really have to be humble if she hoped to remain in his employment. This man was respected throughout the City. He was hardly likely to tolerate his secretary's behaving in such a manner. Verity felt sick again; how on earth was she to face him? She was certainly daunted by him despite her outward behaviour.

'Are you with us lesser mortals, or still on a different plane?' Saul's taunting voice made Verity jump with surprise.

She swung round in her chair, completely flustered, and blurted, 'Do you want me to clear my desk now, and then phone the agency for a replacement?' She clutched the arm of her chair as she spoke, her nails digging deep into the soft leather. She watched him as his face changed from amused mockery to a stern, hard look.

'You have decided to leave, had enough of the old ogre?' he asked almost gently, his granite features strangely at odds with his tone. His eyes dark, his pupils as black as the night penetrated her very soul.

'No!' Verity denied softly. 'I just thought—I mean, in the circumstances——' The flicker of rage that flashed across his face silenced her immediately. She felt her pulse-rate quicken and a feeling of panic beginning to rise within her; she swallowed hard.

'I think we had better discuss this in my office,' he said abruptly, turning on his heel and marching into his inner sanctum. The cold harshness of his voice sent a shiver of fear through Verity's body but, as his actions left her no choice, she followed him in, each step being forced from her reluctant body. But Verity was determined to remain calm. If she was lucky she might be able to hang on to her job; she must not appear to be afraid of him, or she would never have his respect. Maybe as he had already had so many secretaries he was willing to overlook last night, she thought hopefully.

The granite expression on his face soon robbed Verity of that expectation. He stood behind his desk, and his very pose was threatening. His firm legs were set apart, his strong arms folded across his muscular chest. His facial expression was one of bored impatience. He sat down as she entered and began to tap on his leather blotter-pad in a fast beat. Verity faltered for a moment, then, taking a deep breath, she walked stiffly to his desk and stood before him. She swallowed hard as his sharp eyes flashed up at her.

'Miss Chambers,' he barked exasperatedly, 'I fail to understand why you want to leave my employment.'

'Last night I thought that——'

'I had no right,' he interrupted harshly, his ice-blue eyes darkening. 'I was wrong to pry into your personal life.'

'I'm sorry I slapped you,' admitted Verity, surprised by his admission that he was wrong, and feeling quite relieved that she was not about to lose her job. She smiled as she apologised and it lit her face with a youthful vitality he had not seen before.

'There's no need—it's not the first time a woman has slapped my face,' he smiled, treating Verity to the warmth of his smile that set her heart racing.

'Nor the last?'

'I suppose not.'

'And do you always deserve it?'

'Oh, yes!' he laughed wickedly, his eyes bright with delight.

'Then I have no sympathy for you.'

'I haven't asked for it.'

'No,' agreed Verity.

'Though no woman has ever been as lucky as you,' he warned, becoming serious again.

'Lucky?'

'I normally repay such behaviour; in these days of equal rights it seems only fair.'

'I don't believe you!' cried Verity, tilting her head back defiantly, although her voice lacked conviction. He was a man who set his own standards; Verity knew that, and shivered.

'You had better believe me, next time you too will pay the consequences.' He stood immediately as he spoke and moved towards her, stopping less than a foot from her. She could feel his warm breath on her face and she lowered her head to avoid the impact of his steely-blue eyes. The faint aroma of his lemony aftershave wafted towards her and Verity swallowed hard. It was a long time since a man had stood this close to her, and she found herself automatically becoming faint-hearted. She mentally scolded herself. Be strong, demand his respect, she mused, and forced her eyes to meet his. The impact she felt as she looked up into his eyes was like a volt of electricity. She felt uncomfortable; up close he was very daunting indeed—strong, animal-like, but controlled and very careful.

'I think I'd better start work now,' she said sharply, moving backwards away from him.

'Does Hannah remember her father?' Saul asked suddenly, catching Verity off guard.

'Er—no, he's never seen her,' she answered truthfully, disliking her closeness to him and the personal turn in the conversation.

'Then it's time you stopped living in the past and looked to the future,' he said grimly, his eyes sweeping over her body appreciatively. 'It's such a waste.'

'I am not living in the past,' she snapped.

'No? Then why are you so scared? A man has not been this close to you for too long.' He smiled as he spoke, a slow, deliberate smile of seduction. Verity stiffened; the truth of his remark was hurtful and she struck back immediately.

'When you have known a man such as Jonathan everyone else is a poor second,' she retorted, hoping the gibe would hit home. When it did, Verity questioned the wisdom of her remark. He gave the appearance of a man very close to the end of his patience. He ran his hand quickly through his hair and took a sharp intake of breath. Verity longed to move away, but she would not give in; she held her ground firmly, and matched his steely gaze. Yet inside her heart was thudding uncomfortably; he scared the breath from her.

'I have to agree whoever put up with your waspish tongue must have been one hell of a guy.'

'A wasp only attacks in self-defence,' countered Verity, wondering why she and Jonathan had never had conversations like this—she was enjoying the repartee. Probably because Jonathan and I were in love, she thought smugly, trying to reassure herself.

'Self-defence?' he mocked. 'What are you defending, and from whom?' he taunted. Verity coloured at the blatant sexual reference and lowered her head; he made her feel so vulnerable.

'I'll start work now,' gulped Verity, longing to be away from him—far away.

'Are you always so efficient, or are you running away?'

'Yes, I'm efficient and no, I'm not running away.'

'Why, then, are you so eager to work?'

'That's what you pay me for,' she retorted grimly.

'That's right,' he agreed, nodding, but his eyes had narrowed again and Verity felt her legs beginning to tremble with nervousness. She longed to turn and walk away, to tell him that she no longer wanted his job; but her circumstances prevented her doing so.

Feeling trapped and vulnerable, she looked back up at him in silence, her blue eyes dilating at the image before her. He was the fiercest-looking man she had ever encountered. Verity found herself mentally comparing him to Jonathan. He certainly was not as handsome as Jonathan, but there was a rugged attractiveness about him. Jonathan had had a beautifully carved face, though it had retained a softness that Saul's definitely lacked. There was no hint of gentleness in this man's cold eyes, no tenderness, and yet he was, in a strange way, attractive. The contempt and arrogance of the man coupled with his dark piratical features was a fascinating combination. Verity was aware of the physical effect he was having on her, and a shiver of fear rushed through her body. If she was to embark on a relationship again, and it was a big if, then Saul Easton would be the last man she would choose.

'What are you thinking?' he asked abruptly; still dangerously close, his voice had a taunting silky edge.

She regarded him with a composure she did not feel. She wondered why he seemed so determined to intimidate her. She replied as coolly as she could, 'I was thinking how unlike Jonathan you are.'

'The father of your child?' he asked sharply.

'Yes,' nodded Verity numbly.

'And compared to him I am an old ogre,' he stated, then without waiting for a reply he waved his hand in a dismissive gesture and turned away, marching back to his desk, where he sat down heavily and sighed. Verity left the office with her mind in a turmoil and her heart racing. She sat down at her desk, her body trembling, and wondered whether she still wanted the job. She had no idea how long she sat there thinking, but the ring of the phone brought her right back to her senses.

'Ellis and Easton Enterprises,' answered Verity efficiently. 'Mr Easton's secretary.'

'Is Saul there? It's Imogen,' whispered a husky voice.

Verity didn't even acknowledge the caller—the voice was unmistakable. She connected her immediately with uncharacteristic abruptness. The rest of the morning went along quite smoothly—Saul remained in his office and Verity was grateful that she had no need to disturb him. She now had regained her composure and was determined not to get caught again in conversation with him. For some reason she found him strangely disturbing. He *was* an ogre, but she could no longer call him old, when she recalled how young he looked when he smiled... But it was such a rare occurrence, thought Verity; at least smiling at her was, at any rate. By the time Saul called her in she was restored to her usual cool efficiency.

'Miss Chambers, please sit down.' His voice betrayed a concern Verity hadn't expected, so she remained rooted to the spot. 'Sit down!' he repeated as he pushed her into the chair and took up her hand. Verity felt a rising panic inside her. With a blinding flash she knew something was wrong. It was the same tone of voice her father had used when breaking the news about Jonathan. She rose immediately from the chair, her voice shrewish.

'What's happened? It's Hannah!' she cried, her face draining of colour as she spoke and a sickly hot feeling sweeping over her body. She swayed slightly and Saul pushed her back down in the chair and stood in front of it, his body blocking any attempt she might make to move.

'Personnel have just telephoned—Hannah had difficulties, and is in Casualty at the General,' he explained calmly.

'I've got to go to her, she will be terrified all on her own!' gasped Verity, still numbed by the shock, although her instincts made her aware of how poor Hannah must be feeling.

'I'll take you; don't worry, I'm sure she will be all right,' reassured Saul. 'And a schoolteacher is with her,' he explained.

'I see,' nodded Verity numbly.

'Stop feeling guilty; let's just go,' Saul said as he took Verity by the hand and led her out of the office.

Verity was too distressed to even answer. She allowed herself to be ushered into his car and she sank back wearily into the indulgent luxury of its interior. She stared vacantly out of the window, recalling the last time this had happened; her eyes grew soft with the memory, and hot unbidden tears splashed on to her hands.

Please God, not this time, not again, she mentally prayed as they drove in silence to the hospital. Saul took command of the situation immediately and Verity felt almost grateful that he had taken the trouble to show his concern—yet in a way she resented it. She had taken pride in the fact that she could cope without a man— she'd had to—now she wasn't so sure. It was the first time she'd been truly alone, without even her parents for support, and it was hard.

The nurses, like all females, were not immune to Saul's brand of sexuality, and they were more than eager to assist him all they could. Verity mentally registered their envious looks and thought how pathetic they were. If only they knew what a tyrant this man was their opinions would soon change, she thought grimly as they were escorted to the ward. Finally, after a long walk, they were both taken to a small cubicle off the main ward. Verity froze as she stared in horror at her young daughter, her small body barely visible in the large hospital bed.

'Hannah!' she wept, rushing towards the bed and lifting her daughter into her arms, crying softly.

'Hello, Mummy,' wheezed Hannah, sounding remarkably bright and cheerful.

'Mrs Chambers, your daughter is quite all right. She has had an attack of breathing difficulties brought on by a temper tantrum,' said the doctor. 'Does your daughter often hold her breath when having a tantrum? No? This is her first attack, then?' he asked, puzzled.

Verity whispered, 'Yes,' her eyes still fixed on Hannah.

'Is there a family history of asthma or eczema?' the doctor probed, trying to piece together a medical history.

'An asthmatic, yes; I mean, no, I'm not, but her father had asthma,' Verity tried to explain, but the doctor, realising the stress she was under, turned to face Saul.

'It's common in children; most times they grow out of it, as you know. Your wife is obviously distressed, which does not help matters; these things are best ignored. Though naturally the school could not take responsibility. You understand?' the doctor smiled.

'What has caused this?' asked Saul seriously, casting an anxious look towards the bed.

'It could be an unknown allergy, but I'm tending to think it may be due to stress, anxiety, starting school, the mother's return to work—and I'm afraid the child did mention being without a father,' the doctor explained, looking puzzled.

'Hmm, I understand,' replied Saul, nodding in agreement.

'Well, I'll leave you and your wife to discuss matters. A working mother may not be the ideal situation, but women these days...' said the doctor, his disapproval evident in his tone as he left the room, nodding a goodbye to Verity as he left.

'How dare you pretend to be her father?' snapped Verity, her sapphire eyes burning with fury.

'I didn't; he just presumed.'

'But you made no attempt to put the record straight, did you?' Verity almost shouted.

'No, I didn't; I thought it best if she did have a father under the circumstances,' he replied, equally angry, with a violent expression on his ruthlessly carved face.

'What makes you think you would be suitable father material?' sneered Verity, glaring at him.

The look of disgust on his face and his darkening eyes silenced Verity. She had never seen him look so angry before and he terrified her. He stared in silence at her for what seemed an eternity until finally he spoke. Verity stared back with equal hatred.

'If you like, I'll inform her father,' he taunted bitterly.

'No, that won't be necessary.'

'He has a right to know,' growled Saul, his eyes narrowing as they darted from the small figure in the bed to Verity's strained face.

'He's dead,' gritted Verity through clenched teeth, her shoulders sinking at the admission. She was still aware of how close he was to losing his temper, but she kept her eyes fixed upon him, waiting to see his reaction and hoping that it stung. Saul's eyes flickered for a moment, then he forced the breath from his lungs in a low whistle.

'I should have known,' he said, shaking his head in disbelief. 'I really do live up to your image of an ogre, don't I?'

'Yes,' spat Verity, her eyes filled with contempt. 'Now I should like to be left alone with my child,' she added coldly, despising his very presence, and the look on her face left him with no doubts as to what she was thinking.

'I had no idea; if you had said...'

'Why should I have—of what interest could it be to you?' she answered bitterly, the pain of being alone resurging.

'I hope she is all right,' he said as he left, but the concern in his voice was wasted on Verity—she was too absorbed in her own thoughts to heed him.

'Has he gone, Mummy?' asked Hannah sleepily.

'Yes, darling, he's gone,' answered Verity reassuringly, worried that their anger had perturbed her.

'That's a pity—I like him. Don't you, Mummy?'

'Hmm; you rest now,' replied Verity. How could she possibly tell her innocent little child the distaste she felt for that man?

'Do you think he will come again?' the little girl asked innocently.

'I doubt it,' sighed Verity as she tucked Hannah's bedclothes around her.

'He could be my daddy, 'cause I haven't got one.'

'No, darling,' replied Verity, shaking her head, 'he could never be that.' The thought of being married to him made Verity's blood run cold.

Later that afternoon Hannah was discharged; there was nothing physically wrong with her. The difficulties she was experiencing at school had precipitated the tantrum, so an appointment was made with an educational psychiatrist. Verity spent a week with Hannah and her teacher trying to sort out a suitable programme of work that would help her. Verity was reassured that these initial difficulties were not uncommon and she would notice a marked improvement in a matter of weeks. A huge teddy-bear had been delivered to the flat; in his arm was stuffed a curt note from Saul, saying that she could take as much time as was necessary, but, as Hannah was now more settled at school and Mrs Collins was more than capable of looking after her, Verity was determined to resume her position.

The huge furry bear for Hannah was an instant success—she had adored it immediately, much to Verity's annoyance. It was an expensive toy—the type she longed to buy Hannah herself but was unable to do so. It was diffiuclt leaving Hannah that morning—she looked a little flushed and anxious once she realised Verity was going to work and not to school with her.

'You'll be all right, and when I come home you will
be able to show me all your work,' Verity smiled, and
Hannah nodded bravely, then waved her goodbye. Verity
felt she had no option; if she took any more time off it
might result in her losing her job. Verity was already
sitting at her desk typing up some outstanding letters
when Saul arrived. Verity kept her eyes fixed on her work
as he entered. She could feel his cool-eyed observation
of her, but she refused to acknowledge his presence.

'Good morning,' he said coldly, his face betraying
none of the surprise he felt at her being there.

'Good morning, Mr Easton,' replied Verity, still typing
furiously as if her life depended on it.

'My office, now,' he barked as he marched past. Verity
didn't move; the last few days had taken their toll. She
was exhausted with worry and though she had returned
to work the guilt she felt weighed heavy on her shoulders.
She was in no mood for his caustic tone.

'Miss Chambers.' His harsh tone vibrated on the intercom. 'Now!'

Verity was now weary; how dared he command her?
I'm not a slave, she fumed. Verity was angry, and determined to give Mr Saul Easton a piece of her mind.
Not pausing to consider the rashness of entering his office
without first controlling herself, Verity marched in. If
he wanted to fire her he could, damn him! she thought.

'Now,' he said softly, catching Verity off her guard.
'May I ask why you have returned to work so soon?'
His soft tone didn't fool her for a second; Verity bristled.

'I have an income to earn,' she snapped back, immediately on the defensive, as always with him.

'I thought I made it clear that your wage would be
paid and your post remain for you.' His sharp tone

nudged her into alertness. Verity wasn't sure how to answer. Was it her own vanity that had made her return? Was she so determined to be self-sufficient that she was unable to accept help? she mused silently to herself before dismissing the idea.

'I'm waiting, Verity.' The sound of her name on his lips made her visibly stiffen.

'Hannah is fine now——'

'No,' he interjected sharply, his ice-blue eyes chilling even further. 'She is not all right; she has a problem and it's a problem she is going to need help—your help—to overcome.'

'I know that,' retorted Verity fiercely, 'but what do you expect us to live on—fresh air?'

'No; that's why I gave you your full salary—the head-master thought it best if you remained at home,' he explained gently.

'You have spoken to the headmaster?' demanded Verity in disbelief, her eyes wide with amazement at his audacity.

'Yes, I have, and please don't shout at me,' he retorted firmly, his voice low and threatening.

'How dare you? What business is it of yours?' she shouted, not caring what he thought.

His eyes grew dark with pain and anger, and his face was granite-hard as he said coolly, 'I wanted to know how she was, and I knew you wouldn't tell me,' he accused. 'I've seen how you live. It can't help you, working full-time...'

'And you can?' she retorted. She was angry now, furious; how dared he criticise her or her actions? It was all right for him—he had plenty of money.

'I allowed you the option of staying at home with your daughter if you wished. I thought that might be a start but, as you seem determined not to accept it, then I suggest you stop thinking about yourself and consider her.' His voice, though quiet, was disturbingly threatening.

'I do consider her—all the time,' retorted Verity, her sapphire eyes shining with a cold brilliance as unshed tears pricked at their backs.

'Really? Then why are you here?' he said laconically.

'Because I need the job—no, I needed it. Now I've had enough. I've suffered you in silence, but no more, Mr Easton, no more!' yelled Verity.

Then, turning on her heel, she marched straight out of the office. He might have been going to reply, but his private telephone rang, preventing him doing so. Within minutes, Verity had stormed back into his office and thrust her perfectly typed resignation under his nose.

CHAPTER THREE

SAUL snatched the letter from Verity's hand and crushed it into a small tight ball. The aggression of his action betrayed his barely controlled temper. Then he tossed it away in disdain and raised his head swiftly to look at her. His hard eyes, filled with unconcealed contempt, seared through her slender frame. Verity felt her anger beginning to drain away under his cold, calculating gaze. How she regretted her action! She felt totally stupid. What on earth had possessed her to behave so childishly? She shivered as his dark eyes viewed her, but she was locked into immobility like a frightened child.

'If that's your resignation, I accept,' he said in a chilling tone. Verity nodded mutely, too afraid of him to speak. He continued in the same icy tone, 'I do not want you to work a full month's notice. This week while I finalise the Bouvier deal will be quite sufficient for both of us,' he concluded, folding his arms in a gesture of finality. Then he leaned back lazily in his chair, his eyes assessing her body with a cold detachment. Hot anger seared through Verity, the very power of it making her tremble. Her grand act had been well and truly crushed. She glared at him, her cheeks flushed with temper, her sapphire eyes shining with a brilliance they had lacked for so long.

'That's fine by me,' she snapped. 'The sooner the better.' Saul rose from his chair swiftly, his face dark with anger, his eyes narrowed to diamond chips of ice.

He grabbed suddenly at Verity's wrist and she gave a cry of surprise at the crushing strength of his grip.

'I shall expect——' He paused, a cruel smile curving his sensuous mouth, 'No, demand,' he added, 'your respect till you leave my employment.' Verity did not reply, but she matched his gaze with equal strength. 'You do need a reference,' he continued, annoyed by her lack of response.

'Yes,' spat Verity. He raised his eyebrows quizzically but there was no amusement on his face. 'Yes, Mr Easton,' Verity answered, gritting her teeth in anger.

'That's better,' he smiled as he released his grip. Verity was stunned once again by the brilliant charm of his smile, and her stomach flipped uncontrollably, which angered her. She, however, was indifferent to its spell; she knew him too well to be fooled by his cunning charm. Hot tears of rage pricked Verity's eyes; he had humiliated her, and seemed to take delight in her discomfort.

'You may go now,' he said, a wry smile of amusement on his handsome face, his voice cool yet still retaining its authoritative tone. She turned to leave his office, and as she did so he spoke again. 'You're angry—that's a good sign.'

'Whatever do you mean?' queried Verity as she swung back round to face him.

'Anger,' he explained gently, 'is an emotion—not a pleasant one, but it's a start.' His cold blue eyes bored into her, and she felt a tinge of pink on her face.

'I have no idea what you are talking about,' she replied haughtily, but a nagging fear was already pricking at her conscience.

'Despite the fact that you are a very passionate lady,' Verity blushed at his words, 'you have denied yourself.

Perhaps anger is a start. But what a waste,' he concluded, his anger now abated so that he spoke almost regretfully.

'Any emotion spent on you is a waste,' retorted Verity.

'Perhaps, but at least you react to me—that you cannot deny.'

For a moment Verity was speechless; she glared at him angrily, unable to deny the truth of his words. It was true—she had never felt more alive than when she was sparring with him.

'You buried all emotions with Hannah's father; that was wrong,' Saul affirmed, his granite features betraying nothing. She gasped with amazement; was there no end to this man's arrogance?

As calmly as possible Verity spoke. 'Mr Easton, we have to work together this week, and, unpleasant though that is, I suggest we try to retain a professional decorum.'

'Efficient as ever, Miss Chambers.' He nodded curtly.

Not wishing to discuss her private life with him again, Verity did not bother to reply; instead she left his office with as much dignity as she could. Though her mind was in a turmoil, Verity still held her head high, her walk was proud and graceful and did not betray the vortex of questions that were bubbling inside her head. Verity was not looking forward to working her notice; she found Saul Easton far too disturbing. She wanted to establish a solid career, security for Hannah. Now she felt she was back at square one.

This job was the best she'd had; she was using all her skills and enjoying the new challenges. If it had not been for Saul, it would have been perfect. Verity knew that a good reference would make all the difference to her future employment, so, suffocating her natural dislike for the man, she worked well and as professionally as possible. In fact that week was the hardest Verity had ever worked in her life. Saul had never been easy to work for; now he was unbearable. The forced politeness they treated each other to only seemed to add to the tension between them. Even when he was totally out of patience and nothing appeared to be going right he kept up the unfailing act. He never failed to say please or with deliberation tack a pointed 'Thank you' on the end of every request.

Verity refused to show any anger; she remained serene, determined not to show how much he annoyed her. Yet the Bouvier deal was paramount, and Verity used all her skills to ensure it all went smoothly as possible. She took a pride in her work and was determined to do a good job for her own sake despite the fact that it would be Ellis and Easton Enterprises that would gain—and that meant Saul Easton. She was far too professional to let her personal dislike of the man influence her.

By Thursday afternoon she was exhausted, but at least the arrangements were drawing to a close. The City was already beginning to buzz with rumours and Verity couldn't help feeling a thrill of delight, knowing that she had been a very important asset to the deal. Mr Saul Easton was yet again about to make a very calculated move and the City was already applauding his name at the impending result. Verity was still checking the final documents when he entered. He stood staring hard at her for a few moments as if thinking carefully about what he was about to say.

'Miss Chambers, I owe you my thanks.' Saul's quiet voice drew Verity's startled eyes to his. She had not heard him open his office door, and seeing him there, his masculine frame almost filling the doorway, unnerved her. They had not spoken to each other at all except about the office work, and his tone was definitely different.

'Thanks?' repeated Verity blankly. 'What for?'

'Surely you know?' His dry tone was mocking. 'The deal is nearly finalised and without you that would not have been possible; therefore I owe you my thanks.' He sounded sincere but there was a mocking edge to his voice that Verity noticed—the polite façade she had assumed in his presence over the last week was beginning to wear a little thin, and Verity was not sure whether or not he was being sarcastic. She raised her head and her soft blue eyes confronted his cold blue ones.

'I was merely doing my job,' she returned frostily, matching his cold stare.

'And you did it admirably. Thank you.' And with that he brought from behind his back a huge Cellophane-wrapped bouquet of beautiful red roses.

Verity stared in disbelief; she looked up at him, her eyes wide with amazement. It had been so long since she had received a gift, and she was very touched. She felt her heart-rate increase and hot pins pricked the back of her eyes.

'Oh!' she cried in surprise, her cheeks glowing and her eyes filling with tears at such a spontaneous gesture.

'You do like red roses?' he asked, concerned at seeing the tears forming in her eyes.

'Yes, yes, of course I do; it's just so unexpected,' Verity answered. She loved the roses, but why should he suddenly be so kind towards her? Verity's mind began to tick over at a furious rate; she viewed the roses with a growing suspicion. He was not a man to waste any-thing—even this gesture was bound to have ulterior motives, she mused. Then she took the bouquet from him warily and he watched her as she did so, knowing that she was not fooled by his charade.

'And that's not all,' he continued persuasively.

'There's more?' queried Verity, smiling up at him with a note of caution in her voice. He returned her smile ruefully, as if aware of her distrust, and yet his warm smile made her feel strangely vulnerable.

'Dinner tonight—I've already arranged for Mrs Collins to babysit.' His velvet voice was soft and warm; he had moved closer to her as he spoke, and she could smell his pungent aftershave.

She was flustered for a moment and stammered, 'How?' She felt foolish when she said it, and he answered her with his customary coolness.

'The telephone—a wonder of modern technology.' He smiled again, friendly without his usual superior air.

'I'm not sure,' replied Verity. The sudden change in his behaviour towards her was puzzling. Could she really trust him? she wondered, and then, even more to the point, could she trust herself now that his attitude had changed? He was charming, and she had so little experience of men. Jonathan had been her only lover, and she had not even dated a man since his death. Though she did not like Saul Easton, it was pointless to deny that he was a very attractive man. He would know, like a master, exactly how to treat a woman. No doubt an invitation to dinner meant he would want something more, thought Verity anxiously; that's the way it is nowadays.

She began to panic and bit her bottom lip as she thought about the invitation. She would be able to cope with Saul Easton, surely; after they had worked so closely together this week she knew she had earned his respect.

'You will be quite safe, Miss Chambers; I shall make no attempt to seduce you,' he drawled lazily, a smile of superiority on his face showing his amusement.

'I can assure you, Mr Easton, that possibility had not even entered my mind,' Verity replied tartly, but she coloured as she spoke, knowing that it was an untruth. He became serious, fearful of a refusal.

'You have no idea how much it means to me taking over that French company,' he said, a bitterness entering his tone as his eyes darkened for a minute. 'Please come; it's very important and we both deserve a treat.' The hangdog look that he gave Verity made her laugh.

'Yes, I will; what time?' replied Verity, still a little nervous but determined not to let her imagination run away with her, and she didn't want Saul Easton thinking that she was afraid of him. Though he certainly possessed an animal sexuality that would threaten any woman's equilibrium.

'Let's say eight-thirty; but go home now. You ladies take forever to get ready,' he instructed her, his tone of authority evident. He gave a smile of triumph as he turned away, but Verity was unaware of it. Then he returned to his office, still smiling, and took up his pen. Then slowly but quite deliberately, with a great deal of pent-up anger and frustration, he scribbled over the name Bouvier till it was unreadable. A cruel, bitter smile crossed his face as he tossed the file with disgust across the desk . . .

Verity meanwhile had wasted no time; she had left the office immediately, unaware of his actions. She knew going out to dinner with him would mean somewhere very expensive, and she had nothing suitable in her wardrobe. Verity didn't have a great deal of money, so she knew whatever she bought would have to be suitable for a number of occasions. This made her choice a little more difficult, but finally she chose a sleek dark evening suit in a beautiful rich ebony-black colour by Mondi. She paired it with a vibrant red silk blouse that enhanced her colouring, bringing emphasis to her doelike blue eyes and pale complexion.

Then Verity rushed to pick Hannah up at school. Hannah ate her tea slowly while Verity listened to a full record of today's events. The little girl was certainly happier at school now, and inviting a schoolfriend home to tea once a week was a help. Verity really felt that things were going well. She was grateful when Mrs Collins came to take her into her flat for a while, as it gave her time to get ready. Verity, despite herself, was excited; it was so long since she had been out, and she was determined to enjoy herself. She washed and conditioned her hair and put it up into rollers while she took a bath. She applied her make-up with care, giving emphasis to her natural beauty. When she was happy with the result she began to loosen her hair. It fell around her shoulders in thick dark natural waves—a perfect foil to the clothes she was wearing, and she teased the curls softly till they framed her face. She then dressed slowly, allowing the fabrics to fall against the natural contours of her body with ease. To complete her outfit she wore pearl stud earrings. When she finally looked in the mirror she knew, like every confident woman, that she looked stunning. When the doorbell rang she just had time to spray a little perfume on her neck and wrists before answering the door.

'Good evening, Miss Chambers,' Saul smiled, revealing his beautiful white teeth, his eyes noticeably widening with surprise at seeing the transformation—but he said nothing. Verity felt a stab of anger for a moment, then quickly brushed it away; of what interest was it to her what he thought of her?

'I'll just say goodbye to Hannah,' said Verity, calmly aware of the effect she was having. He had obviously not appreciated how good she could look. She walked serenely across to the other flat, knowing that his eyes were following her every move. Mrs Collins was equally amazed at the result of her preparations for the evening.

'Verity,' she gasped, 'you look beautiful!'

'Don't sound so surprised,' laughed Verity; then she turned her attention to her daughter and kissed Hannah goodnight. Hannah, though, was more interested in Saul; her eyes were fixed on him in wonder, and Verity felt a stab of guilt because she knew how much having a father would mean to her. She hugged her daughter even tighter, trying to give double the amount of love in one embrace. Once she was settled perhaps she would go out more, thought Verity; maybe she could love again...

She was so wrapped up in her own thoughts that she hadn't even noticed that they were outside. It was the cries of the children that shattered her thoughts. She looked up at once to see Saul's sleek expensive car parked in the small quadrangle, looking completely out of place among the older shabby cars. Several children had gathered around it and were peering into its windows and commenting on the personalised number-plate. Verity felt a little self-conscious as he opened the door; it all seemed very unreal to her. The car was the epitome of luxury living; when she had ridden in it before she had been too distressed to notice. It had deep burgundy leather upholstery, and a stereo system that put the tinny record player Verity owned to shame. Saul sped off into the dark night air, an excited air about him and a secret smile on his face.

Verity watched him from the corner of her eye. Call it female intuition, but there was definitely something going on, she mused. Though she wasn't sure what, she knew enough about Saul Easton to know that he wasn't to be trusted. It was some time before they reached the hotel; it was as plush and luxurious as Verity had imagined it would be. She was pleased that she had spent the time and money on her outfit. Her usual clothes certainly would have looked out of place. They had spoken to each other on the way, and Saul, though preoccupied with his own thoughts, was politely attentive. He escorted her towards the reception desk, where a smiling, over-anxious manager stood waiting. Verity stiffened when she heard the manager say the rest of the party had already arrived. She darted a quick look at Saul, but his only reply was a slow smile. He then took an uncomfortably firm grip on her hand and escorted her over to the solid oak door.

'What's going on?' she asked, puzzled, her instincts telling her that her idea of a private dinner was wrong. She was annoyed by Saul's apparent deception and her own naïveté in believing him.

'This, hopefully, is the final act; after this the contracts should be signed,' he explained, looking earnestly at Verity.

'This is business, not dinner!' she exclaimed, her eyes flashing.

'It's a cocktail party and I desperately need you here,' he pleaded as Verity turned to leave in disgust.

'Why did you lie; why couldn't you just ask?'

'Would you have come?'

'I don't know—I doubt it,' she answered honestly.

'I do need you here—I must have this contract.' The strength of conviction in his voice perturbed Verity.

'Why bother with the roses? I should have known they were a bribe.'

'They weren't,' he snapped. 'I did want to thank you, but tonight, well, I just thought you would feel out of your depth at a cocktail party and you would refuse to come.'

'What do you mean, out of my depth?' replied Verity, bristling.

'Seeing you tonight, I realise I was wrong, but I...' He faltered for a moment.

'Mr Easton, we are here now; I suggest we carry on with this farce. Thankfully by this time tomorrow I will no longer be in your employment.' Verity's icy tone was chillingly sarcastic.

'Efficient as ever.' He gave her a curt nod as he opened the door. Verity smiled, a sickly sweet smile.

'Well, thank you, Mr Easton.'

'Saul, and may I call you Verity? It's less formal.'

'Of course; that is the correct procedure at such occasions, is it not?' replied Verity, still angry at the deception.

'Yes, and please, Verity, be the perfect hostess. I need you. You have no idea how much this means to me,' he said, his ice-blue eyes fixing on her almost pleadingly.

'I shall be on my best behaviour.' She smiled, enjoying the power she had over him.

'I need you tonight but remember you'll need me tomorrow—you'll need references if you hope to gain employment again.' His voice was quietly threatening, the strength of his grip tightening momentarily. She could feel the unleashed power in his hold, and for a second she was a little afraid.

'*Touché*!' replied Verity, raising her head swiftly, her dark eyes confronting him with a sparkle of amusement. Yet he was not amused, and stared back at her stonily. The room was large and seemed to be full of people all milling around pretending to socialise when all they talked about was business. Verity idly picked up a glass of chilled white wine from the tray that was offered to her and quickly scanned the hall. A small band was playing, its soft tones drifting gently around. Verity took a sip of her wine and nodded her head in appreciation.

'Château Bouvier, no doubt?' she queried.

'Correct, but soon it will bear a different name.'

'"Easton" hardly has a ring about it.'

'I said it would have a different name—not my name.'

He had moved closer to her as he spoke, and Verity was aware of the effect she was having on him. She could feel his cool blue eyes travelling ever so slowly over her curvaceous outline. He did not appear to miss an inch, and when his gaze finally reached her face he smiled warmly without any embarrassment. A tingling sensation had spread throughout Verity's body. She took a steadying breath and met his gaze head-on. There was no mistaking the aura that had been instantly charged between them. Verity was unable to stop herself staring into his calculatingly hypnotic eyes. The spell fortunately was broken by the Gallic tones of a mature man.

'*Bonsoir*, Saul—I was wondering what kept you; now I know!' His English, though excellent, still betrayed his accent.

'Good evening, Mr Bouvier. May I introduce Verity Chambers, my secretary?' Saul said.

'*Bonsoir, Monsieur Bouvier; enchantée de vous connaître,*' said Verity as she extended her hand. Verity's accent was perfect and Saul's eyebrows rose in surprise.

'*Enchanté, mademoiselle,*' he replied, raising her hand to his mouth and kissing it gently. '*Vous êtes très charmante.*'

'*Merci, vous êtes gentil,*' responded Verity, knowing that this type of exchange was always expected by the French. Saul watched with growing pleasure. Verity was aware of his feelings and knew that his pleasure was in the thought that if they continued to get on this well with Bouvier the contract would be his.

Saul left them to talk; his tall muscular body wove effortlessly, despite his size, through the jostling crowd. He cut a swath through them, confident that he was going to succeed. A grim smile curled his lips cruelly as he viewed the photographs of the Bouvier estate. He had never wanted something so badly before. Then he turned and looked back at Verity. He had been mesmerised by her all evening. She had certainly taken him by surprise. Where was the little wallflower he'd employed? Tonight she had certainly blossomed. Her dark hair alone would attract attention, but when it was coupled with her pale features and her deep blue eyes she really was stunningly beautiful.

Verity certainly was enjoying herself. It was stimulating talking the language again. She had travelled ex-

tensively in France when she was a student, so it was a
natural choice when she'd decided to become a bilingual
secretary. Mr Bouvier was captivated by her; he was an
oldish man, well into his sixties, but he had retained his
attractiveness despite his age. Verity was enjoying his
company, but she was relieved when Saul rejoined them;
it was difficult to keep talking French, and the strain
was beginning to tell.

'Thank goodness you came back,' whispered Verity
as Mr Bouvier moved away and began to talk with
another guest.

'You seemed to be doing all right; what's the
problem?' enquired Saul. He had inclined his head to
hear what she had to say and still kept it close. He really
was a powerfully attractive man, admitted Verity reluctantly as she moved away slightly. He looked up and
smiled, the same devastating smile that pierced into her
very being. Verity became flustered as she tried to meet
his gaze head-on. She could feel her own eyes widen in
response to him, and cursed her body's betrayal.

'You look beautiful tonight,' he teased, knowing that
she was already embarrassed.

'I know; the Frenchman has used all his Gallic charm
and has informed me several times over,' she remarked
coolly, yet her heartbeat had increased at his compliment.

'Is it so long since a gentleman gave you a compliment
that you do not know how to react?' He moved closer
as he spoke, his cold eyes fixing on her, his powerful
stare forcing her to look at him.

'I didn't realise you were a gentleman,' she retorted,
matching his look with equal determination. Though she
felt far from safe. He had been watching her closely all

evening with a rakish air, and Verity had been aware of him the whole time.

'Tut, tut,' he said, shaking his head. 'I'm not, but there again a lady wouldn't mention the fact.' He grinned mischievously as he stepped nearer in a threatening manner, his unleashed masculinity sending a thrill of excitement through Verity's body. He raised his hand and with slow deliberation stroked the outline of her face. His touch was like a jolt of electricity. Verity stiffened; she knew her face had flushed at his touch. She tried to compose herself but her heart was thudding uncomfortably against her chest, her pulse racing. She took a very deep calming breath and swallowed hard. She smiled serenely at him, disguising the feelings she had inside.

'Mr Easton, no doubt a man with your reputation is more than capable of attracting the attention of many females—the scent of money is incentive enough for most. Please play your little games with them. I am here only in the capacity of your secretary, and I find that loathsome enough.' The look on Saul's face at these words was surprisingly tranquil. His eyes, though, had darkened and his voice was so frosty that his breath almost chilled the air.

'I like a challenge. And what makes you have such an abhorrence of money when you have so little—or is that why?' Saul contained his anger remarkably, thought Verity as she looked him squarely in the face.

'I have my reasons for distrusting people with wealth, and you only compound them,' Verity answered, thinking about poor Jonathan. She had thought more about him this last month than she had done in years.

'Miss Chambers, try and keep a civil tongue in your head—at least for tonight,' Saul reprimanded her, his eyes narrowing and a fleeting look of anger crossing his face. But Verity felt bold, knowing that he needed her here tonight so badly that she could say anything. Certainly the expensive wine had instilled her with confidence.

'I'll try, Saul, I'll try; but I can't promise,' she said airily, waving her hand dismissively as she sauntered away. She could feel his eyes boring into her back, but she was undaunted. He had tricked her, used her talents for his own ends—even tonight had been a deception. It was so typical of those people with wealth—they always thought that their money gave them certain rights over others. Verity felt a searing anger growing inside. She hated Saul Easton and all he stood for. She sat down near the window and looked across the well-lit lawns, thinking about all her tomorrows. She still needed a reference from Saul, but that was the only power he had over her. Then an idea struck her. Perhaps Monsieur Bouvier might have a business friend who would have a suitable vacancy for her.

She stood immediately, her excitment mounting as the idea took shape. She would go and ask him right now; it was obvious that he was impressed by her. It was almost definitely the wine that had instilled her with such confidence, and she marched over the room determined to find suitable employment by her own merits, not by the opinion of Saul Easton.

'Monsieur Bouvier,' she said politely, smilingly demurely as she spoke. Verity swallowed hard, then, taking her courage in both hands, she enquired if he knew of anyone who might have a suitable vacancy for her. He turned and looked at her, his eyes bright with amusement, and began to laugh.

'A lovers' tiff, *ma petite*?' he asked, like an indulgent parent. '*C'est vrai*, Saul is madly in love; he would never let you go.'

'Oh, no, you have misunderstood; I am Mr Easton's secretary, nothing more,' explained Verity quickly, wondering what on earth had given him the impression that she and Saul had anything but a business relationship.

'*Ma chérie*, you English are so staid, but my eyes do not deceive me. Saul has watched your every move all evening,' he informed her, pleased that he had spotted their clandestine rapport.

'No, honestly,' pleaded Verity, but she knew it was falling on deaf ears. Of course Saul had watched her all evening—this deal was so important to him that he wasn't going to allow his secretary to upset the proceedings at this late stage.

'Ah, Saul, your secretary here is telling me she wants a new position—maybe wife, *n'est-ce pas*?' Verity coloured immediately as Saul swung round, his eyebrows raising in surprise.

'I want a new position, but certainly not as his wife,' Verity snapped at once.

'Young love…' said Bouvier, shaking his head. 'You would be foolish to let her go,' he added to Saul, and smiled indulgently as he pushed them together. Then he scurried away under the impression that the lovers wanted to be alone. Verity's soft breasts fell against Saul's hard muscular chest before she could stop herself.

He wrapped his strong arms firmly around her shapely body as she tried to move away.

'Release me or I'll scream!' spat Verity through clenched teeth.

'Don't be ridiculous; if he wants lovers, I think we should oblige. The contract has not been signed yet,' he informed her, his grip tightening. Verity's heart was beating almost uncontrollably; she knew he must be aware of it. Her body had stiffened in his arms and her eyes blazed with anger.

'Release me now or I shall ruin any hope of the deal being signed,' she threatened venomously. Though she wasn't sure how she would be able to. Saul's arms fell immediately to his sides. He stared grimly at her, his face cold with anger, his eyes narrowing to ice-blue flints. He was controlling his anger remarkably well, but Verity knew how close he was to losing his grip on it.

'I need this contract—no, not for the money; I have other reasons,' he confessed. 'I am willing to do anything to achieve that end.'

'You may be, but I'm not, and nothing could induce me to be your lover,' she said fiercely, moving away from him as she spoke.

'You promised you would help me,' he retorted, his eyes brilliantly icy, his hard muscular body still too close for comfort.

'Promised!' scoffed Verity. 'I promised nothing; this whole evening is a deception from beginning to end. The only reason I remained was because of your threats.'

'Here,' snapped Saul angrily, taking a white envelope from his pocket and thrusting it into Verity's hand. She opened it slowly and stared at the contents in disbelief. He had already typed an excellent reference; it was full of praise yet retained a dignity and truth. Then she noticed the cheque; it was handsome by anyone's standards. Verity faltered for a moment, unsure what to do. Then, much to Saul's surprise, she took up the cheque and with slow deliberation she tore it smartly in half while her eyes remained fixed on him.

'Mr Easton, I shall not be bought, not at any price.' The calmness in her voice surprised Verity herself, as her nerves were jangling as she spoke.

'That was as a reward for all your help—not a pay-off,' he growled.

'Really—as the roses were to say thank you and to-night was dinner?' she replied sarcastically.

'Would you believe me if I apologised?'

'I suppose not.'

'Then it's pointless to do so.'

'Try it, Mr Easton,' Verity goaded.

'I am sorry...' He paused; the words did not come easy to him—but Verity was in no humour to be generous. 'I've been carried away with this deal,' Saul continued. He certainly did sound contrite but, as he had just confessed that the deal meant everything to him, was he to be believed? mused Verity thoughtfully.

'Are you sorry, really sorry?'

'Yes, I am. Perhaps the best way to convince you is for you to leave now. You have your reference, so just go,' he commanded, a steely edge to his voice.

CHAPTER FOUR

'I THINK I believe you, despite everything, I do,' said Verity emphatically. Saul visibly relaxed and expelled the air from his lungs in a low whistle, his relief evident.

'Thank you,' he smiled as he extended his hand in a gesture of friendship. Verity took his hand; his grip was strong and warm and dark hairs grew untidily across the back of his hand. She felt a stirring disquiet at his touch and raised her eyes to look at him. He, too, was staring at her. Verity immediately blushed and dropped her hand from his grip.

'Why is this deal so important?' she asked, hoping to steer the conversation to neutral territory.

'I enjoy wine, so why not own a vineyard?' he laughed, and Verity smiled in return, but it was hardly a sensible answer.

'Are there going to be any changes?'

'No, I shall leave them well alone; but I am now the sole owner of the estate and as such could make sweeping changes if I wanted,' he said confidently as he sipped his wine.

'There were other vineyards for sale; I did comparisons on them all. The Bouvier was not the best——' began Verity, but he raised his hand to silence her.

'I wanted the Bouvier estate, and after tonight it should be mine. The reasons why I want it are immaterial.' His voice was cold and dismissive; whatever his reasons were he was not about to tell Verity. Verity frowned and, not wishing to upset her, Saul immediately suggested they look at the aerial photographs of the vineyards. They were both poring over the pictures when Mr Bouvier joined them.

'*Non*, this is not the way of lovers,' he laughed, amused by the interest they showed in business. Verity looked embarrassed but Saul smiled broadly, slipped his arm around Verity's waist and drew her closer to him. She could feel the hardness of his body against hers, the smell of his pungent aftershave assailing her nostrils. She tried to move but Saul tightened his grip immediately and held her firm.

'We were just admiring the vineyard,' confessed Saul, as he prodded Verity. She responded immediately and began to flatter Mr Bouvier.

'Yes, it really is beautiful.'

'*C'est vrai, c'est très belle.*' He enthused at length about his beloved country, then he snapped his fingers. 'Aha! I have an idea—perhaps it would be best if the contract was finalised in France. One cannot grow wine without love in one's soul,' he explained, grinning widely.

'I thought you were willing to sign tonight if——' Saul began anxiously.

'France—at the vineyard; it is only right that we exchange contracts there,' Bouvier said, aware that he was in control.

'When?' snapped Saul, determined not to lose.

'Why not on Monday—you are both free then, *n'est-ce pas*? You shall be my final guests before the château becomes yours.' Bouvier's voice was firm. He was determined to have the contract finalised in France. 'There among the sweet-smelling vineyards, warmed by the sun, you shall become true lovers again!' He grasped them both by the hand and smiled triumphantly.

Verity darted a swift look at Saul, but he chose to ignore her.

'Of course we shall be delighted to attend; a few days away will do us both good.' He smiled warmly as he accepted the offer, but made sure his eyes did not meet Verity's.

'Mr Bouvier, I feel——' she began.

'You feel as delighted as I am,' interrupted Saul, his voice bright but his eyes sending out warning messages. Verity concurred for the moment. She had no intention of going to France, and even Saul Easton could not make her. She waited patiently till Mr Bouvier left then she turned abruptly and faced Saul.

'I am not going to France,' Verity stated simply, trying to remain calm.

'You must; he expects us both. It is imperative that you attend.'

'I am not going,' Verity repeated, her voice raising an octave.

'The deal will not be signed if you don't go; you must come,' he hissed, not wishing to be overheard.

'I leave your employment as from tomorrow, so I will not be going to France.'

'But he thinks you are coming.'

'And who gave him that idea? You. So now you can explain to him that I shall not be attending.'

'You must come!' growled Saul, taking her harshly by the shoulders and forcing her to look at him. He was desperate, and losing control. His eyes were like chips of flint as he stared at her, barely concealing his wrath. His grip had tightened on her shoulders and Verity could feel his strength beginning to hurt her. She gave a cry of pain as his hands dug deep into her shoulder-blades. At once he released his grip, as if only then he was aware of his actions. He looked shocked.

'I'm so sorry—I had no idea; are you all right?' He sounded really concerned and anxious.

'I'm fine,' replied Verity coolly, her contempt for him evident in her eyes. She turned to go, but his hand stopped her.

'I am sorry; I wasn't thinking. Verity, please, I didn't mean to hurt you.' She stopped; there was something in the way he spoke her name that made her. She turned and looked at him.

'Mr Easton, I've no idea why this contract is so important to you, and frankly I'm not interested, but you can count me out.' Then she turned away from him and left the room. Once she was outside, the cold night air chilled her blazing temper, and all that was left was an empty, cold feeling of desolation.

Next morning Verity walked briskly into the office humming quietly to herself. She hadn't realised just how much stress she had been under the last few weeks, and now a marvellous sense of relief filled her. Today she would finish working for Mr Easton and as it was the mid-term break she had decided to take the whole week off and spend it with Hannah. Maybe the finances would even stretch to a few days by the sea, thought Verity as she began to clear her desk. It seemed odd to be leaving; though she had only worked here a short time it seemed an age. In a strange way, she mused, I've almost enjoyed the strenuous workload, but Saul Easton... Verity shuddered. She was amazed by the amount of rubbish she had collected in her desk in a matter of weeks. There were old magazines, empty crisp packets from snatched lunches, even a mouldy apple had taken root in the corner. Verity turned her nose up in disgust as she tried to dislodge it, then tossed it into the waste-bin. There was hardly any work to do—just a couple of letters and a little filing. She was determined to finish both in record time and leave before having to face Saul.

'Miss Chambers, if you're not too busy I should like to speak to you.' His silky voice taunted, fully aware that there was no work to be done. Verity felt herself bristle at once; his arrogant attitude was even apparent in his voice. It took a considerable effort to present a relaxed façade as she walked calmly into his office.

'Ah, Miss Chambers, I was wondering if you have reconsidered——?'

'No, Mr Easton,' Verity interrupted sharply with scant attempt at civility. 'My answer remains the same; I will not be going to France.' There was a flash of irritation in his eyes then his lids lowered carefully, masking his anger. He tapped his strong, lean fingers relentlessly on his desk as he sat deep in thought.

'Is that all, Mr Easton?' Verity goaded, a smile of satisfaction on her face.

'No, it is not all,' he corrected with cold anger, a freezing contempt gilt-edged in his dark eyes as he stood to face her. Verity felt her stomach set up a frightening whirl of butterflies as he approached her, yet she was determined not to weaken. She glared at him fiercely, her head tilted back so that she could look him directly in the eyes. The tension welled up between them, thundering in her veins as his sharp eyes burned into hers with compelling intensity. Verity swallowed as he stood before her, silent and threatening. She felt her resolve weakening and forced her eyes to remain fixed on him. His jaw tightened at her defiant expression, and his eyes changed to a forbidding ebony.

'You have to come; this deal depends on you. You must realise that.' His voice was quiet but there was a steely edge to it, warning Verity that he was barely controlling his formidable temper.

'I am not going,' Verity replied simply, amazed by her own composure when her insides were a mass of nerves.

'You will; you have to.' His voice was quiet and menacing, and Verity felt a shiver of fear run down her spine.

'Are you threatening me, Mr Easton?' asked Verity icily, her eyes betraying her fury. His equanimity was not shaken in the least by her accusation. His dark brows rose slightly to let the glimmer of arrogant amusement shine from his dark eyes. He shrugged his powerful shoulders lazily.

'Threatening you? Of course not. I want you to come with me.' He paused, then added with a cold finality, 'and I always have what I want.'

'Then this time, Mr Easton, you will be disappointed,' snapped Verity as she turned from him and marched out of his office. Verity snatched up a piece of paper and fed it huffily into her typewriter, then she pounded away on the keys, her fingers furiously expressing her anger at his arrogance. One hour later Saul asked her into the office again.

'Have you changed your mind yet?' he asked, a mocking smile curling his sensuous mouth. Verity felt her heart skip a beat as an unaccountable feeling stirred within her. Automatically she smiled back and shook her head.

'I'm sorry; the answer is the same.'

He grinned by way of reply and nodded his head as in acceptance, knowing that would be her reply. It continued for the rest of the day every hour on the hour; he called Verity into his office and asked her the same question, and each time he received the same reply. Finally it was five o'clock, and Verity was getting ready to leave when Saul appeared. He stood just inside the doorway, his taut muscular body framing it completely.

'Leaving me already, without so much as a goodbye?' he asked, smiling. Verity turned to face him; the warmth of his smile made the blood rush through her body, making her tingle. She felt a flush of colour on her face as she tried to regain control of herself.

'Of course I was going to say goodbye,' she flustered, suddenly aware of the attraction she felt for him, and relieved that she was leaving his employment.

'Were you?'

'Yes.'

'Well?'

'Goodbye, Mr Easton.' Verity extended her arm as she spoke, but knew instinctively that she was taking a chance. He took her hand firmly, his touch scorching her, and she tried to draw it back immediately. His grip tightened as he drew her towards him. There was a deep, slumberous warmth in his eyes, and his mouth was relaxed, curved into a soft inviting smile.

Verity lowered her head; she was not going to allow him to kiss her, but her body was betraying her and she felt herself fall against his hard chest. He lifted her chin till her face met his. Then, with slow deliberation, his mouth gently moved against hers. The touch of his lips pierced her body like a shaft of fire burning deep within her. Verity began to respond despite herself, then, as the realisation hit her, she stiffened and became passive. He immediately drew back, looking faintly amused by her reaction. There was a trace of mockery in his voice as he spoke.

'Goodbye, Miss Chambers.'

'Goodbye,' answered Verity as she made her way swiftly through the door without looking back. Her heart was still racing and her face was flushed. She leaned against the wall outside and let the chilled air cool her. She took a deep breath, trying to regain her composure, and for some unknown reason she felt so alone she wanted to cry.

The incessant ringing of the doorbell awoke Verity. She turned over and smiled at the small sleeping form that lay rolled up in a ball beside her. She stroked Hannah's hair softly before stealing away to answer the door. Verity opened it to be confronted with the daunting form of Saul Easton. Verity gasped in surprise and her heart thudded as he directed her a slow, lazy smile.

'Can I come in?' he asked, his sensuous mouth widening to show his beautiful white teeth.

'I'm not dressed,' replied Verity, pulling her thin towelling robe tighter around her as Saul's eyes travelled over her body with obvious desire.

'Evidently,' he drawled, his mouth curling into a sensuous smile. Verity felt a rush of colour across her face as he stepped closer. The closeness of his body was electrifying, and she felt naked before him. Verity stepped backwards, almost falling over Hannah's toys, but Saul's strong arms surrounded her immediately, drawing the pair of them together. Verity's heart leapt and a strange sensation darted through her body. She wanted to protest, but any objections died on her lips as she looked up and found herself hypnotised by his dark eyes gazing into hers. He released her gently but the power of emotion had now charged the atmosphere and Verity felt powerless. Saul looked bemused by Verity's obvious discomfort.

'I've had an idea,' he began confidently.

'Really? And I suppose it has something to do with France?'

'How did you know?' he laughed, and the familiar smile sent Verity's heart pounding.

'A lucky guess.'

'Let's make it a holiday; bring Hannah—it would do her good,' he added persuasively. He had sat down, but his muscular body still seemed large and daunting in the small flat. Verity shook her head.

'No.'

'What?'

'It's a simple enough word, Mr Easton—no!' she said firmly. Saul shot to his feet, alarming Verity with his agility.

'You can't mean that,' he laughed, so confident that his offer to take Hannah would make the trip acceptable. Verity was annoyed by his self-assurance; with her eyes blazing she marched over to the door and opened it.

'Goodbye, Mr Easton,' she called, turning, but Saul had settled himself back into the chair, with a languid look on his face, his arms resting on the back of his head.

'Let's talk,' he coaxed. 'I'm sure I could persuade you.'

Verity stared in disbelief; a flush of colour suffused her face and her sapphire eyes shone with a cold brilliance. 'Out, now,' she stated coldly, pointing to the door.

Saul arose panther-like—there was an animal strength in his relaxed manner that was quite daunting, and Verity felt a shudder of fear down her spine; she was all too familiar with Saul's temper. He came closer and closer, his eyes fixed on hers, but she stared resolutely back, determined not to give in. He stood facing her, his taut muscular body framing the doorway. He raised his hand and Verity took a sharp intake of breath. Then very, very gently—almost tenderly—he pushed a tendril of hair from her face. Verity's heart was racing, and the pair of them stood facing each other. Suddenly the anger mingled with another element which sent her mouth dry.

'Mummy, I woke up and you had gone.' A sleepy-voiced Hannah stumbled out from the bedroom rubbing her eyes, unaware of the spell she had broken.

'Good morning, Hannah, it's half-term now, isn't it, and you have a full week off school? Maybe you would like to come on holiday with me to France in an aeroplane?' Saul said immediately. Verity knew now that she was beaten; before she could protest Hannah had gleefully accepted and was skipping around smiling broadly.

'Don't look so cross; you'll enjoy it. I'll make sure you do, I promise,' Saul said sincerely as he looked at Verity's grim expression.

'Everything is just so easy for you, isn't it? Do you think I or Hannah have the type of clothes suitable for a holiday? At this time of year all the shops are full of winter clothes.'

'I'm sorry, truly I am. This deal is just so important to me that everything else was forgotten. Please let me help you.' Saul took hold of both of Verity's hands as he spoke with such genuine warmth and sincerity that she nodded in silent agreement. It was pointless to fight this any more; he had won, but at least he was not gloating about it.

The rest of the day was a whirlwind of shopping, Sunday was spent packing suitcases, and it was with great relief that Verity finally sat on the aeroplane awaiting take-off. Hannah was so excited that she was silent for once as she stared out of the window in disbelief while the aircraft lifted off the ground and began its ascent. Verity watched her anxiously, not knowing how her young daughter would react to the flight.

'Relax, she's fine; I want you to enjoy yourself, re-member,' warned Saul as he passed her a glass of cham-pagne he had ordered. Verity raised the glass to her lips. It seemed so unreal to be sitting late on Monday afternoon sipping champagne while flying over the Channel. Obviously Saul was used to such events, as he seemed totally at ease. Verity tried hard to enjoy herself, and the task was made all the easier by Hannah's en-thusiasm. In less than two hours they were being driven down the country lanes of France towards their desti-nation. Verity gave a cry of delight as the endless rows of vineyards gave them the first glance of the château. It not only lived up to its photographs—it surpassed them.

'An enchanted castle!' laughed Hannah delightedly as she pointed in wonder to the building. Her childlike ob-servation was silently assented to by both adults, and even Saul seemed to have a smile of supreme satisfaction on his face. He brought the car to a smooth halt outside the main door; it opened immediately and a pair of energetic hounds bounded out, barking furiously. Monsieur Bouvier followed, his arm outstretched to greet them as if they were old friends. Hannah viewed the dogs warily and when one ran up and tried to lick her she burst into a flood of tears. Verity turned to comfort her, but was too slow—Saul had already swept her up in his strong arms well out of the dogs' reach. Hannah's chubby arms wrapped around his neck with obvious delight, and Verity felt a stab of jealousy at her daughter's open display of affection.

'Ah, she is a daddy's girl, *n'est-ce pas*?' nodded Monsieur Bouvier. 'Please take her up to her room—it is adjoining yours; Madeleine will show you the way.'

As if by magic a plump housekeeper appeared, smiling broadly. Verity stiffened; surely she wasn't expected to share a bedroom with Saul? She tried to attract his attention, but with a cool deliberation he turned away and followed the housekeeper up the winding stairs to the top turret. Verity followed, watching her daughter's head slowly fall slavishly on his broad shoulders.

'Saul, she's asleep; put her down gently on the bed and she won't wake up,' whispered Verity in his ear, aware of the intimacy of this shared moment. The housekeeper disappeared, informing them that Raoul would bring up their luggage directly. With careful manoeuvring Saul and Verity managed to place the sleeping Hannah on the bed without her waking.

'She must be shattered, emotionally drained after the flight,' laughed Saul softly as he gazed at the curled-up form of the little girl with a wistful, tender look in his eyes. Verity slipped the sandals from her daughter's feet, gently drew back the covers, and placed her inside. Verity looked at the sleeping form with a smile of satisfaction;

she was pleased she had come, at least for Hannah's sake.

'Just look at this view,' Saul called from the small balcony. He swept his arm out in an expressive gesture. 'This will soon be mine. Thanks to you.' He drew Verity towards him and an alarm bell immediately sounded in her head. She pulled away quickly, her heart racing when she spoke, although she was amazed at the calmness in her voice—it certainly belied the turmoil she felt inside.

'Whatever Monsieur Bouvier wishes to believe is his affair, but I hope you don't have any illusions; we are not lovers, we shall not share the same bed.'

'Your loss or mine?' he mocked.

'I'm serious; where are you going to sleep?' There was a tremble in her voice as she spoke, but she remained calm.

'So am I; for God's sake, Verity, you can't go on living in the past. You can't exist on memories.' His tightly controlled voice jerked her and she turned away. 'I've no intention of forcing you to do anything, but for your own sake you have to start living again,' he continued with searing logic.

'And I might as well start with you, is that it?' she sneered, her eyes blazing in temper. He shook his head resignedly.

'No, I wasn't offering myself as an antidote for this torch you carry round, but face up to reality: he is dead, and you're alive—at least half alive.' His voice seemed cold, cruel and hard. Verity tried to run to escape from his harsh accusations but he was too quick for her; within seconds she was trapped in his arms. Grabbing her roughly by the shoulders, he twisted her around in his arms till she faced him.

'I have Hannah—she is my life,' she protested weakly as the truth of his words penetrated her.

'Hannah's life is her own too; don't try to live your life through her—it's not fair to either of you,' Saul countered, his dark eyes fixed on hers with compelling intensity. Verity stared at him, sapphire eyes bright with moisture.

'Saul, please; I'm tired, so tired.' She struggled again fruitlessly in his strong arms.

'Don't you think I know that?' he growled but, though his grip lessened, he did not release her. 'Life is far too precious to waste, Verity.'

'Yes,' Verity replied dully, wishing he would just leave her alone.

'Damn you, Verity!' he exclaimed, shaking her shoulders fiercely, as if trying to arouse her dormant emotions, his voice loud and strident.

'For goodness' sake keep your voice down—you'll wake Hannah, and what on earth will the rest of the household think?' Verity spat in a freezing tone, her sapphire eyes shining like diamond chips.

'A lovers' tiff, no doubt,' sneered Saul as he drew her closer, his strong arms enveloping her body and making escape impossible.

'Get your hands off me!' hissed Verity through clenched teeth as she threw back her head defiantly, her dark hair falling across her shoulders in a heavy mantle. She felt trapped, too vulnerable, and she panicked, as if another layer of her armour had been shattered, and she felt threatened by his proximity. The warmth of his body was scorching her skin. He said nothing but held her even tighter.

The silence that followed frightened Verity more than the noisy exchange of words. She looked up and their eyes became locked in a silent conflict. Verity drew back her head in alarm as his change of expression registered with her. She could see the devilish lights flickering in his ebony eyes. He took up her hair in his fist, and pulled it back till her face was upright. She watched transfixed as his dark head descended till her vision became blurred. She was locked into immobility, then the slow, painful awakening began. An exquisite longing immediately struck deep within her very being. Feelings that had been denied for so long. Her whole body became alive with expectation, tingling as his soft mouth began his punishing onslaught. She trembled as her defences began to weaken and crumble.

She longed to respond; her arms instinctively began to reach out, but she fought against the desire. She needed so much to hold him, to feel his hard muscular chest against her was becoming an overwhelming desire. Yet she could not afford the luxury of responding, so she remained totally passive. He began to caress the nape of her neck with slow, careful precision, applying gentle pressure then releasing it. The soothing effect of this massage was too much for Verity and she began to kiss him. She wrapped her arms around him, pulling him even closer to her. She dug her nails deep into his back as his probing tongue eased her mouth open, forcing his hot lips on hers in a sea of desire. Then, as they seemed to reach a pinnacle, just as Verity was responding with careless abandon, he stepped back, releasing her, aware of how she felt. He gave her a slow, mocking smile.

'You're more alive than I thought,' he stated with droll cynicism. 'I'd better sleep in Hannah's room,' he said as he picked up his case and went silently into the adjoining room. Verity waited till she heard the door close, then hurried over and turned the key in the lock. Saul gave a wry smile as he heard it. The atmosphere was charged with energy and as the pulsating excitement ebbed slowly away Verity felt even more weary. She leaned back against the door, her heart still racing, her mind a vortex of unanswerable questions. She sighed and pushed her hair from her face, suddenly becoming aware of her bruised, tender lips. She went to the mirror and stared in disbelief at her mouth; it was swollen and sore. She touched it with her fingers, softly stroking where his lips had been.

'Damn you, Saul Easton! Damn you!' she cursed at her reflection. She bowed her head as hot tears fell from her eyes. The situation was impossible; she shouldn't have come, and now she was here there was no escape. The tears of mixed emotions flowed freely till Verity could cry no more, then, with her characteristic strength, she wiped her eyes and decided to take a shower. There was no way she would let Saul Easton know what effect he had on her. The warm, pulsating water cascaded over her slender frame, easing the tension from her body.

Hannah slept on, allowing Verity some precious time to make herself feel better. She decided to dress soberly to reinforce the idea that she was here in an offical capacity. She chose to wear her new navy Alexon suit with a pure white linen blouse. She scooped her hair up high in a fashionable chignon and secured it carefully. Make-up as usual was kept to a minimum, but a slight gloss on her lips was essential to cover the bruising left by Saul's harsh kiss. She shuddered at the memory; he had kissed her without the gentleness or consideration that

Jonathan had, and yet even the memory of his lips seemed to arouse greater emotion.

It was another half-hour before Hannah too was ready to go down, by which time Verity had managed to regain her usual composure. Saul and Monsieur Bouvier were seated outside in the shade of a beautiful pergola that was covered in a blanket of vines. Fresh plump grapes hung in large purple bunches from every branch, filling the whole area with their pungent scent.

'Verity,' smiled Saul warmly, rising immediately with his catlike agility. There was a wicked glint in his eyes as he wrapped his arm around Verity's waist and steered her to a chair. Verity stiffened at his touch, and so he leaned closer and whispered in her ear, 'He expects lovers, remember.' His hot breath caressed the side of her face and Verity could only nod dumbly in response, but her eyes flashed out a silent warning to Saul.

'Ah, whispering sweet nothings—it is the way of lovers,' laughed Monsieur Bouvier, pleased to be part of their intimacy. Verity coloured, ashamed of the deceit, but powerless to do anything.

'The vineyard is now mine; we await your signature as a witness, that's all,' said Saul, a triumphant note in his voice. Verity smiled sweetly as Hannah reached out and plucked a small bunch of grapes from the vine.

'You had better ask Mr Easton whether you can have them,' laughed Verity as she signed her name with a flourish. 'He is now the proud owner.' Verity gave Saul a mocking smile as she passed him the document back.

'Of course you can have them—there's plenty.' And he reached out and took one from the bunch. He turned to Verity and held out the grape to her mouth. Though she disliked the intimacy of his action, she obediently opened her mouth and he popped in the ripened fruit.

'Monsieur Bouvier and I are going to have a walk down to the presses; why not stay here and enjoy what's left of the sunshine? I'm sure Hannah would rather play with the workers' children than follow us around,' Saul informed her as he rose from his chair.

'Thank you, I will,' nodded Verity, pleased to have the chance of some peace. She closed her eyes and allowed the soft, flickering shadows of the leaves to soothe her gently into a drowsy slumber. Hannah had called out that she was playing with Suzanne and, confident that she was safe, Verity allowed herself to fall into a relaxed sleep.

'*Bonsoir, mademoiselle. Ça va?*' The strongly accented voice woke Verity from her slumber immediately. Her eyes shot open to face an extremely attractive man. His olive-tanned skin was emphasised by the stark whiteness of his short-sleeved T-shirt. His arms were criss-crossed with a mat of curling dark hairs which failed to conceal the physical strength in his muscular arms. Thick dark brows emphasised the deepest blue eyes that Verity had ever seen, and the long curling lashes that surrounded them would have been the envy of every woman.

'*Bonsoir, monsieur...*' Verity paused with her arm extended in greeting.

'Bouvier—Étienne Bouvier.' He drew her towards him as he spoke, and kissed her lightly on both cheeks in the Gallic fashion. Verity felt herself colour, and he laughed. '*Vous êtes Anglaise, n'est-ce pas?*'

'*Oui, c'est vrai,*' Verity confessed, knowing that her handshake had revealed her nationality even though her accent was perfect. He sat down, his long legs stretched out in front of him, totally relaxed, and he picked idly at the grapes, eating each one with a bored detachment. It was so relaxing to be in the company of someone so easy-going after the pressure of working with Saul that Verity talked freely. Étienne listened with interest and spoke proudly of his country's capital—Paris—where he lived in the spring. Verity had never been to Paris, and to hear it described by a true Parisian brought the city to life. They were deep in conversation when Saul returned, their laughter, which filled the evening air, making them unaware of his approach.

'Étienne.' Saul's voice chilled the cosy atmosphere immediately, an indescribable look of victory chiselled into his hard features.

'Easton!' spat Étienne in response, jumping to his feet immediately, his face registering his incredulity.

'It is you—my father has sold to you!' It was an angry accusation underlined with a hidden hatred. The slow smile of triumph filled Saul's face, but it lacked warmth, and his eyes remained fixed on Étienne with a cold brilliance. Verity's eyes darted from one to the other, but they both seemed unaware of her presence. They were locked in a conflict she knew nothing about, but the charged atmosphere was apparent enough.

'I would never have agreed to the sale had I known,' thundered Étienne, an almost hysterical note in his voice. Saul shrugged his powerful shoulders in a careless fashion, enjoying the other man's discomfiture.

'But you have expensive tastes—you needed the extra money,' he sneered, his eyes glinting with amused malice.

'Not your money, Easton,' the Frenchman hissed back, the tendons stiffening in his arms as if he was ready to fight. Verity watched the two men, silently mesmerised by the unleashed anger they were both trying to control.

CHAPTER FIVE

MONSIEUR BOUVIER left later, but Étienne seemed determined to stay.

'Surely you can't resent my staying? I would be your guest,' Étienne mocked Saul, taking delight when the latter's face darkened.

'I can't imagine why you should want to remain,' snapped Saul, viewing him with suspicion.

'Ah, well, there now is an added attraction.' He smiled mysteriously as he passed Verity, but Saul remained stony-faced. The atmosphere at dinner was a little strained, to say the least, though the food was flawless—artichokes with béarnaise sauce, then a rich coq au vin served with sorrel salad and a Camembert with fresh pears for dessert. A burgundy from the vineyard was served throughout the meal, but Verity made sure she drank little; she wanted to keep a clear head with Saul being so close. Hannah was taking her meal in the kitchen with Madeleine's children, so there was none of her constant chatter to cover the embarrassing silences. Saul sat grim-faced, despite the fact he had succeeded in securing his deal. Étienne, though refusing to talk to Saul, was delightfully attentive to Verity.

'Your eyes are the colour of sapphires, and shine with the glint of diamonds,' he said charmingly to Verity as he escorted her, his hand falling gently around her slim waist. He pulled out the chair next to him. Verity felt herself colour with pleasure, and Saul gave a snort of laughter. Étienne turned to look at him briefly then turned his attention on Verity.

'I see Saul does not appreciate your beauty, but then, Saul never did appreciate women.' There was a taunt in Étienne's voice directed at Saul, but he kept his eyes fixed on Verity. Saul's face darkened and a fleeting flash of anger swept through his dark eyes. Verity felt sure there was going to be a row, but he remained silent.

'Tell me, Verity, how long have you known Saul?' enquired Étienne, attentively gazing at Verity as if no one else in the room existed, his dark eyes looking over the rim of his glass directly at her. She smiled in return.

'Oh, not long; I have been working for him for over a month,' she replied honestly. Étienne nodded thoughtfully, a smile of satisfaction on his face. He darted a quick look at Saul.

'Really? I thought your relationship was...' he paused significantly '...deeper than that.' Verity felt a flush of colour cover her face, she was so embarrassed. She darted a quick look at Saul, but he stared back, his expression unfathomable. Verity dropped her gaze immediately, feeling—what? Disappointed? Surely not. She smiled brightly, trying to steer the conversation to more neutral ground.

'We are staying here the week, Étienne; I'm sure Mr Easton will be busy. Perhaps you know of local places we could visit?' Verity asked innocently, unaware of Saul's look of disapproval.

'We? Who is this "we"?' Étienne queried with a puzzled look on his handsome face that made Verity laugh.

'My daughter—Hannah—she is here with me.'

'*Une fille?*' he gasped. '*C'est impossible; vous êtes trop jeune.*'

'*C'est vrai,*' laughed Verity, pleased that he considered her too young to have a child. She knew he wasn't that serious, but it was nice to have a little flirtatious fun.

'I too have a daughter, but unfortunately, with my business commitments, I see little of her.' The sense of loss in his voice was apparent, and Verity felt herself instinctively reach out and touch his hand. He placed his own warm hand on top and squeezed it softly.

'Business commitments!' snorted Saul.

'It is true,' retorted Étienne, glaring at Saul.

'Sure!' stated Saul. The tension between the two men seemed to be growing, and Verity felt trapped in the middle.

'I am quite sure Étienne makes every effort to be with his child,' reassured Verity, ignoring the look of black fury on Saul's face.

'You are very understanding,' the Frenchman said with a gentle nod. Verity felt her senses quicken at his touch, his male magnetism attracting her and making her feel sharply conscious of her femininity. Yet despite that she was aware of Saul's presence and could feel his displeasure in his brooding silence.

'Saul is uncle to a child, aren't you, Saul?' Verity said in an attempt to bring the men together on the normally neutral ground of children.

'Are you?' asked Étienne, his eyebrows raising in surprise.

'Yes,' continued Verity, unaware of Saul's steely gaze, 'practically every day a picture or small piece of work is faxed to his office.'

'How touching!' said Étienne, a mocking smile playing on his lips. 'It's a pity you never became a father.'

Saul stood immediately with such force that his chair fell to the ground; he lifted his brandy to his mouth and drank it in one mouthful.

'Goodnight,' he spat at them both with such hatred in his voice that Verity trembled.

'Is he always so charming?' laughed Étienne, replenishing their glasses.

'I've known him in better humours, but they're rare,' admitted Verity, but she could not help but feel that Étienne had goaded him in some way.

Verity, despite Saul's obvious disapproval, enjoyed Étienne's company. Saul was far too preoccupied seeing the workings of the vineyard to have time for sightseeing, so Verity spent her time with Étienne. He was kind, attentive and charming, and he spent the next three days giving Verity and Hannah an absolutely marvellous time.

Every day they went on a trip somewhere; some days Étienne would arrive with a beautiful French-style picnic already stowed away in the rear of his flash sports coupé. Fresh crusty sticks of French bread with dark, coarse, thick pâtés, soft-running local cheeses, an abundance of fresh fruits and the obligatory bottles of chilled Chablis. On other occasions they would eat lunch in a little bistro, sitting at the table outside, enjoying the last few days of warm sunshine before winter drew in.

'Anna! Anna!' called Étienne, unable to cope with the pronunciation of the H. 'Anna, look, I have brought you a present.' Verity frowned.

'Really, Étienne, it is too much; you buy her a present every day—she will be spoilt,' said Verity, trying to sound cross.

'Little girls should be spoilt; if her own father were here, he too would spoil her, yes?'

'No, well, maybe. Look, I don't know!' laughed Verity, unable to stay cross with him when his intentions were so well-meant.

'*Ce n'est rien*,' he said, producing a tiny box from his pocket and presenting it to the eager Hannah.

'Thank you,' said Hannah politely. Enjoying all the attention, she opened the box to reveal a tiny chocolate heart with her name carefully iced on the top. She looked studiously for a moment then popped the chocolate whole into her mouth.

Verity gasped, 'Oh, what a waste!'

'*Voilà, pour vous.*' Étienne extended his hand with a similar box, offering it to Verity.

'For me?'

'*Mais oui.*'

'*Merci.*'

'It is my pleasure; it is so long since I have been in the company of such a charming female,' he replied sadly. 'I am a failure; my marriage is over. I am divorced, but it takes so long to recover from such a loss. It is like a death, is it not?'

'Oh, I'm terribly sorry,' gasped Verity, her arm reaching out to touch him, drawn by a mutual bond of lost love. He turned to her and smiled, shrugging his shoulders expressively.

'*Maintenant*, let us go on a boat down the river,' he cried, and Verity slipped her arm through his in a gesture of friendship. The day was perfect; Étienne had hired a small motor boat and they cruised around the waters till dusk. It was totally relaxing and they made their way back to the château somewhat reluctantly.

'I have taken a liberty,' confessed Étienne on the journey back. 'I hope you do not mind.'

'What is it?' asked Verity, concerned that he was so serious.

'I have asked Madeleine to look after Anna so that I may have the pleasure of taking you out to dinner. Please say yes,' he pleaded.

'That's very kind of you, Étienne. I shall be delighted, but I'm afraid I have nothing really suitable to wear,' admitted Verity as she mentally went through the collection of outfits she had brought.

'Why gild the lily? Your serene beauty needs no ornaments.' He spoke sincerely, nodding his head sagely, and Verity glowed with pleasure. They entered the château, with their arms linked together in friendship, laughing over a shared joke, Hannah following behind, to be met by a grim-faced Saul. His features looked even more forbidding as his jaw hardened when he saw them. A dry cynical smile curved his sensuous mouth.

'I was going to take you out today; despite your lack of commitment, I've managed to finish the work alone,' he snapped, fixing his flint-sharp eyes on Verity.

'Étienne took us on the river,' explained Verity rapidly, aware of the unbroken tension that still remained between the two men.

'I'm not interested where he took you,' Saul barked, his face dark with fury.

'I came here on holiday, remember? That was our agreement,' retorted Verity sharply.

'I will see you later, *ma petite*,' smiled Étienne, gently raising her hand to his mouth and kissing it. He strode away, taking Hannah with him, leaving Verity to face Saul. She could feel the anger bubbling up inside her; how dared he spoil a perfect day by his rude behaviour? Verity looked at him, her eyes bright.

'If you needed my assistance you should have told me,' she stormed, outraged by his behaviour. 'But it's not that, is it?' she challenged. 'It's Étienne.'

Saul's faced clouded at her words and he fixed his eyes on her, but remained silent.

'I have no idea what is between you and Étienne, but since his arrival he has done everything to make me and Hannah feel welcome,' she snapped.

'I bet he has,' he growled.

'What do you mean by that?' retorted Verity indignantly, pushing her thick hair from her face in a gesture of annoyance.

'Oh, grow up, Verity, I know him. Why on earth do you think he is spending all this time with you?' he replied harshly, taking a step closer to her as he spoke.

'He is kind enough to want me to enjoy my stay here.'

'Don't be naïve; the man has a terrible reputation. You're merely the next notch on his bedpost,' he snarled.

Verity coloured with embarrassment. 'How dare you?' she flustered. 'Do you have to judge all men by your low standards?' Her heart was racing as she spoke and as the colour drained from Saul's face she realised she had gone too far. There was a nerve throbbing at his temple, his face had frozen, his eyes had darkened to a forbidding ebony.

'You're a fool—a silly girl with no experience who can't see danger when it's staring her in the face!' he stormed.

'Leave me alone. Étienne is a gentleman; he has never tried to take advantage of me—unlike you!' she added venomously, and she turned on her heel to go to her room.

'Stop right there!' snarled Saul, and his voice was so threateningly quiet that Verity froze despite herself. He grabbed her roughly and swung her round to face him. 'It is because I'm a gentleman that the door between us has remained closed; but don't be too confident, Verity. It would take more than a door to keep me out,' he growled.

'Rape? Is that what you're referring to?' she countered, angry at his arrogance. He gave a cruel jeer.

'No, my dear—I'm quite sure you would be a willing partner,' he mocked softly as he stroked the outside of her lips with cold precision. She shivered as his scorching touch seared her body, and despised herself for her body's betrayal. 'We are leaving tomorrow, early. Be ready,' he growled. Then, as she ascended the stairs, he spoke again. 'Stay away from Étienne; I'm warning you.'

Verity flew up the stairs, wanting to put as much distance between her and Saul as possible. She slammed the door of her room and gave a sigh of relief as she leaned against it. The warning he had given her only made Verity all the more determined to spend time with Étienne. She was delighted that they were going out to dinner that evening, and decided to dress with special care. She chose a soft, full white top with short sleeves and a matching flared skirt. She added white high-heeled sandals which gave her extra height and grace. The few days in the sun had coloured her skin to a honey-brown, so she smoothed a scented oil into her skin, giving it a silky glow. She brushed her hair till it shone and fell over her shoulders in a sheet of darkness against the whiteness of her clothes. She carefully applied a little make-up—a small amount of eyeshadow exaggerated the beauty of her eyes.

In less than an hour she was ready, and taking up her handbag, she hurried down into the kitchen to check on Hannah. There was no need—Hannah was completely at home with Madeleine's children, language being no barrier. She returned to the sitting-room, where she paused at the door and peered round. There was no one there except Saul.

Verity watched him through the crack in the door, a mounting feeling of trepidation growing inside her. She wondered about the wisdom of her action, and remembered the threat he had made. She shivered involuntarily, but what right had he to dictate to her? Verity thought, determined to do exactly what she wanted. Saul was pouring himself a drink as she entered, but he turned as the sound of her heels clicked against the tiled floor. He saw her and seemed to do a double take, his eyebrows raising in surprise.

'Would you like a drink?' He did not smile, but his voice seemed more normal than before.

'Have they a white wine there?'

'Of course.'

He turned to pour her a drink from the well-stocked cabinet that included a fridge for wine. He passed it to her and she crossed the room and sat down near the open doors, allowing a cool breeze to fan her face.

'Are you going somewhere?' he asked innocently, his eyes drifting over her body appreciatively. The suntan certainly added to her looks.

'Yes, I am,' she replied guardedly; there was no need for him to know. She lowered her eyes on her glass. Saul looked at her, his eyes for a moment fully alert, concentrating on her face.

'Where are you going?'

Frowning slightly, Verity replied, 'I'm going out to dinner.'

'May one ask who with?' He was goading her, and she could sense his anger despite the coolness of his questions.

'I don't see what it is to do with you,' snapped Verity, feeling trapped, and her confidence draining away under his perceptive scrutiny.

'Étienne.' He spat the name venomously at her.

'Yes, Étienne. What's wrong with that?' she said, rising from the chair swiftly, wanting to get away.

'He is married; does that not bother you?' countered Saul, outraged.

'*Was* married; he and his wife are divorced. It was very painful for him—he's only now beginning to pick up the pieces of his life,' Verity informed him, pleased that Étienne had confided in her. A cruel smile played on Saul's mouth.

'And you believe him?' he asked sarcastically.

'Yes, I believe Étienne,' she answered, and as she spoke his name he entered, smiling broadly, as if aware of the trouble he was causing and taking delight in it. He presented Verity with a corsage of white flowers with his usual Gallic flair.

'Thank you, Étienne.' She smiled graciously and planted an affectionate kiss on his cheek as she stole a glance at Saul's reaction. A freezing contempt glittered in his dark eyes, his face was set starkly, his mouth was tight and compressed. Verity shuddered and once again questioned the wisdom of her actions. She knew that sooner or later she would have to face Saul alone, and the thought did not appeal to her. Verity tried to put the thought of Saul's wrath to the back of her mind, but it was difficult and, despite Étienne's charming company, the gourmet food and excellent wines, the evening was marred for Verity by the shadow of Saul. Finally the evening was at an end; Étienne was no longer staying at the château, but he drove Verity back, bringing the car to a standstill outside the main doors.

'Thank you for a lovely evening, Étienne; I'm so sorry we are leaving tomorrow,' confessed Verity, toying with her flowers.

'We shall meet again, *ma petite*, perhaps in Paris?' He took the flowers from her hand and tucked them behind her ear. Then he clasped her face and kissed her very gently at first, his warm lips soft and persuasive. Some time elapsed before his kiss became more passionate and his hands started to wander.

Verity drew back and said firmly, 'I'm going now. Thanks for a lovely evening.' Then she got out of the car immediately, leaving him no chance to stop her.

'Thank *you*, *ma petite*; *au revoir*.'

Verity stared after the car as it drove away down the long, winding path, then she turned to enter the château. The moon was suddenly hidden by a cloud, and at that moment Verity heard a branch snap.

'Who's there?' she called nervously into the darkness, and as the moon re-emerged she gave a cry of recognition. Her eyes fixed on Saul, standing tall and powerful in the shadows; his shirt was open to reveal the dark column of his throat, his sleeves were rolled back to just above the elbows. Moving a little closer, she could see the savage look in his eyes, and instinctively drew back.

The silence that rose up between them was charged with electricity. Then Saul broke it by saying thickly, 'Did you have an enjoyable evening.'

'Yes, thank you,' answered Verity, trying to make for the door; but he was much too quick for her, and with animal agility he sprang forward, blocking the entrance.

'Especially the last part? I'm surprised it only ended with a kiss,' he sneered, his hands tightening into white fists as he spoke, as if he was fighting the desire to strike her.

'It was harmless enough—a kiss between friends,' answered Verity in an attempt to make light of the situation.

'Harmless? I wonder whether his wife would agree with that?' Saul taunted, his eyes darkening with anger.

'I told you, their marriage is over, they lead separate lives,' Verity explained quickly, but she felt increasingly vulnerable, alone outside with Saul in this terrible mood.

'You naïve fool. Can you really be that stupid?' He laughed; a cold, cruel laugh of derision that chilled the night air. Ordinarily Verity would have hesitated before she spoke, but her own rage was too great and she was much too furious to care.

'I hardly think you're an expert when it comes to marriage; your own wasn't that much of a success. How long? Less than twelve months, wasn't it?' she jeered, enjoying the stunned look on his face. Then, before he could react, she pushed past him and flew upstairs to the sanctuary of her bedroom.

Verity slept badly that night; she was ashamed of her own remarks, which she knew were unnecessarily cruel. She awoke early with a headache threatening, a dull ache deep in the base of her neck that even a cool shower didn't remove. She packed hurriedly, constantly cross with Hannah, who was reluctant to leave. Breakfast was a silent affair; neither she nor Saul spoke, and Hannah, aware of the unpleasant feeling, remained equally sombre.

'If you're ready I should like to leave directly after breakfast,' Saul said, the chill still evident in his voice. Verity nodded dumbly, unable to look at him directly; last night's events were still etched clearly into her mind.

'Our flight isn't till this evening—I have a call to make beforehand. A personal visit,' he added by way of explanation.

The day was hot, the sun already high in the sky. Verity frowned and searched unsuccessfully for her sunglasses. She had already taken two aspirin, but the pain in her head was increasing, the hot weather only adding to her discomfort. Hannah was noisy as usual, and though Verity tried to remain patient she finally snapped when Hannah screamed out, 'Mummy, Mummy look at the cows!' Her voice pierced Verity's ears, making her grimace in pain.

'For goodness' sake, Hannah! Stop shouting!' she yelled, her eyes heavy as the weight of her head became almost unbearable. Saul tensed immediately as Hannah burst into a flood of uncontrollable tears.

'There was no need...' he began, ready to correct Verity's outburst, when he noticed how ill she looked. He swore softly as he took in her pale visage as she sat deadly still at the side of him. He wasted no time; reassuring Hannah, his voice warm and strong, he thrust the car into fifth gear and began to roar down the road. He pulled in sharply at the service-station and jumped out of the car.

'Come on, Hannah, there's a good girl. Let's go and get a Coke. But quietly,' he added, his voice taking on a firmer tone. Hannah smiled and Verity felt a stab of misery, knowing how well her daughter responded to the dominant male.

'And you; come on,' he said, helping Verity from the car. She stood gingerly holding her head, and swayed slightly. 'You look awful,' he stated matter-of-factly.

'Thanks,' replied Verity, swaying again as a feeling of nausea swept over her.

'Come on—carefully now,' Saul ordered gently, his arms wrapped firmly around Verity, supporting her while his eagle-sharp eyes kept a close watch on Hannah. Verity swallowed in an attempt to fight the desire to be sick, the colour completely draining from her face as she did so.

He glanced down at that moment. Verity heard him call her name, but it seemed distant and faraway; even the tone was gentle and caring—almost unrecognisable. Then she remembered nothing but the suffocating—but welcoming—darkness. When she came round, Verity found herself being carried along, her head resting on his chest. For a moment she stayed still, taking in the scent of his woody aftershave and the feel of the cool, clean freshness of his crisp white shirt. She felt secure against his strong frame, and relaxed... She closed her eyes, drifting for a moment. Then some built-in instinct rang the alarm and she started immediately.

'What's the matter?' he asked, his dark eyes betraying a momentary concern till he lowered his lids, masking his emotions completely.

'Put me down; I'm fine now,' she answered. There was a tremble in her voice but she was unsure whether it was due to her fainting spell or the proximity of Saul. His animal magnetism was hard to deny. He obliged instantly, placing her carefully down in one long gracefully strong sweep.

'Thank you.' She smiled gratefully, relieved that he hadn't insisted on being truly macho and marching through the service-station with her in his arms. The thought alone made Verity colour with embarrassment.

'Ah, at least you're getting your colour back a little,' he mocked gently, knowing full well the reason for it. Verity found it very disturbing that he seemed to be able to read her mind with such apparent ease. Maybe I'm transparent to him, she thought. What did he call me last night—'a naïve fool'? Maybe he's right, she thought. Compared to Imogen I suppose I am.

'Can I have my Coke now, please?' asked an anxious Hannah, tugging at her mother's arm as she pleaded with her.

'Yes, you run on and get a tray,' instructed Saul. 'I'll make sure she sits down somewhere nice.' Verity allowed herself to be steered into a corner seat looking out over the flat countryside. Her head ached mercilessly, the pounding quite the worst she had ever experienced.

'Here, eat this,' commanded Saul, placing a tray of breakfast before her.

'I can't possibly,' Verity said, shaking her head negatively.

'You can and you will—now.' Saul's tone of voice brooked no argument and Verity picked up the fork reluctantly and began to force small amounts of the fluffy omelette into her mouth. She was pleasantly surprised at just how tasty it was. Saul watched her intently the whole time. She could feel his eyes upon her, and looked up once or twice, but his expression was unfathomable and she immediately dropped her gaze.

'I feel better now,' lied Verity.

'Well, you certainly look a little better, but not that much,' countered Saul with an amused light in his eyes.

'We'd better get going; come on, Hannah, drink up,' Verity said, and then stood holding the table for support as the room began to spin uncomfortably before her.

'You'd better take my arm,' offered Saul, gallantly striding over to her and taking her arm in his. Verity gave a weak smile as her stomach turned at his touch.

She must have fallen asleep in the car because the next thing she registered was the cry of delight as Saul got out of the car. Verity watched as Saul bent down and scooped a young child high up into the air and swung her around. Then he was showered with kisses and hugs which he returned with equal enthusiasm.

'Solly! Solly! I've missed you so much!' the little girl cried, tears of joy springing to her eyes, and she clung to him as if she would never let him go.

'My Heloise,' he laughed, kissing her again before setting her down and turning his attention on the car. He faltered for a moment then gave a half-smile. Verity was intrigued; he opened the car door and Hannah clambered out, rushing to introduce herself to her new-found friend. Verity made her way more gingerly; she still felt ill, though her head was aching less since her sleep. Two other adults had come out of the house now—an old couple in their early sixties. They too greeted Saul warmly, then turned to be introduced to Verity.

'Verity, this is Marcus and Charlotte Ellis, Heloise's grandparents.' They all shook hands warmly; Verity noticed a momentary look of surprise on Charlotte's face, but it was quickly gone.

'You look tired, Verity,' Mrs Ellis commented, a perturbed look on her face.

'Yes, she is; perhaps she could take up the guest room for a while?' asked Saul.

'No, no, that won't be necessary—honestly,' interjected Verity, but she found herself outvoted, and was escorted to a small room at the back of the house. Mrs Ellis closed the blinds quietly, leaving just a ray of light shining through.

'Rest for as long as you want, dear; I know what it's like travelling with a small child. It's enough to give a saint a headache,' she laughed sweetly before closing the door. The room was cool and dark, the old oak bed was made up in crisp white linen too inviting to resist. Verity slipped off her sundress and sandals and slipped between the sheets. She sighed, 'This is heaven,' before falling into a deep, much-needed sleep.

It was a lot later when she awoke, and the house was silent. Hannah! thought Verity immediately, pulling on her dress and slipping her sandals on. The house appeared empty, and as she passed each empty room Verity's panic increased.

'We're here, dear,' called Mrs Ellis, and Verity followed the voice to outside, where Mr and Mrs Ellis were both sitting.

'Let me get you a drink—something long and cool,' Mr Ellis said, immediately rising. Verity smiled gratefully as her eyes darted round the beautiful garden.

'Where's Hannah?' she asked, her distress apparent.

'Saul's taken both of them down to the gardens— there's a play area there, and a small boating lake. She's bound to enjoy it,' Mrs Ellis reassured her kindly.

'I see—no, that's fine; I just worry,' confessed Verity, giving a half-laugh.

'Of course you do, it's only natural,' the elder woman replied brightly, but her eyes were dark with an unspoken sorrow.

'Have they been gone long?'

'Hmm, I suppose since you came, really. They don't get much chance to see each other, so they tend to make the best of it when they do,' Mrs Ellis explained. Mr Ellis came back at that moment, leaving Verity intrigued.

'Here's your drink, young lady. Well, you're his new secretary, are you? Tell me, how is the old place? A damn sight busier since I left, no doubt!' He laughed at this remark good-naturedly and sat down, easing his bulky frame into a wicker chair.

'I understand—you're the other half of Ellis and Easton Enterprises!' Verity gasped as the truth dawned.

'That's right.'

'So Heloise is Saul's daughter,' Verity said. The silence that followed made Verity wish the ground would open up and swallow her.

'No,' sighed Mrs Ellis. 'I only wish she were; no, Heloise is my daughter's child, though we tend to look after her—with Saul's help,' she added. Verity smiled and longed to know more, but the conversation drifted off into another direction, leaving her none the wiser.

'Mummy!' cried a voice, breaking into her thoughts. 'We're back!' Hannah bounded up to them, full of confidence, a ready smile on her small face. Saul walked slowly behind, a reluctant Heloise trailing after him. He raised his eyebrows in the direction of Heloise, and her grandmother responded immediately.

'Come on, now, Heloise,' she cajoled, trying to sound cheerful. 'You know this was only a flying visit, but Saul will be here again soon. Won't you, Saul?' she asked, looking at him for reassurance.

'You bet; and you can send me a message every day. I keep all your drawings,' he said seriously, squatting down to face the child.

'You do, really—all of them?' she asked eagerly, desperate for reassurance.

'Indeed I do,' he answered emphatically. 'Don't I, Verity?' he asked, turning his attention to her.

'All the pictures, and the little stories—we look forward to them,' smiled Verity in response. Heloise smiled broadly and Saul rose; a momentary sadness flickered on his face but he masked it almost immediately.

'It's time we were off; I'll be in touch,' he said to Mr and Mrs Ellis. 'Come give me a kiss goodbye,' he said, opening his arms wide for the eager little girl to rush into. Verity took Hannah by the hand and made a discreet exit, nodding her thanks to Mrs Ellis. She sat in the car waiting, her mind in a turmoil. Where was Saul the ogre, the tyrant? He was certainly none of those to that little girl.

'Did you have a good time?' said Verity to a sleepy Hannah.

'Yes, but I wish I had a daddy like Heloise's; he's nice.' Then she snuggled down in the rear seat and closed her eyes.

Saul appeared at that moment. His face dark and forbidding, he strode over to the car in long, purposeful strides, but just as he reached the car a voice cried out, 'Solly, Solly!' and a tearful Heloise came racing towards him. She flung her arms around his legs and clung to him; the heart-rending sobs choked Verity as she watched. Mrs Ellis appeared in a rush and pulled her away.

'I'm sorry, Saul; she realised you had gone,' she explained. Saul jumped into the car immediately, having given Heloise one last peck on the cheek. He started the car at once and roared off. Verity glanced back at the sad little figure that stood forlornly waving a weak goodbye. Then she took a side glance at Saul; his face was set in hard, angry lines, his mouth was tight and compressed, but his eyes were slowly filling with tears. Verity stretched out her hand timidly to his, almost expecting rejection. She gave it a gentle squeeze.

'Are you all right?' she asked quietly. He remained silent, then gave a nod; his eyes remained fixed on the road ahead. He was still driving fast as if the devil himself were in pursuit of them . . .

CHAPTER SIX

VERITY frowned; why on earth had she agreed to come back? She must have been insane. She put the call through and sat glaring at the intercom. How she hated that Imogen; she hung around Saul like a lap-dog and, what annoyed Verity even more, he seemed to enjoy her company. She resumed her typing, her fingers pounding away on the keys.

'Verity.'

She jumped at the sound of his voice, coming through the intercom. They now called each other by their first names, but that was his only difference. They had resumed to treating each other with the cool indifference they'd achieved before the trip to France.

'Yes, Saul?' For some reason she jumped and her heart-rate increased whenever he spoke her name.

'What's the matter? You sound on edge,' Saul soothed mockingly.

'Nothing.'

'Come in, please; I have some letters to dictate.' The intercom became silent and Verity started at it. Sighing, she picked up her pad; it was so easy for him, she thought crossly as she stood smoothing her skirt automatically.

'Tell me, what's wrong?' Saul asked as she approached his desk with obvious reluctance.

'Nothing; why should there be?' she replied, but her mind screamed out, Yes, everything—everything is wrong, and I don't know why.

He smiled, that smile which transformed his face and pierced into Verity's soul, giving it light and breath.

'Really? I thought—— *No* . . .' he paused ' . . . I know there is something wrong.' He kept his eyes fixed on her, but Verity immediately lowered hers in case her confused feelings were evident. 'Well, what is it?' he asked, his voice taking on a cooler tone as he ran his long fingers through his raven hair. His brow furrowed as he watched her.

'Personal,' lied Verity, hoping to stop the conversation.

'Not Hannah again?' he asked so concernedly that Verity felt guilty.

'No, no, not Hannah; she is fine now—settled at school—she's fine, honestly,' Verity continued, hoping he wasn't going to pursue this line of conversation.

'OK. It's just that you seem a little on edge, that's all.'

Verity gave a weak smile and sat down; he smiled back and her stomach flipped. Stop it, stop it! she wanted to scream at him, but instead she took the dictation with her usual composure, masking her feelings with her efficiency.

'Is that all, Mr Easton?' she asked, rising from her chair. He frowned, his eyes darkening.

'Back to Mr Easton, are we?'

'A slip. Sorry. . .' she paused before speaking his name '. . . Saul.'

'Do you find it so difficult to call me by my name? I have no problem with yours——' he hesitated '—Verity.'

The sound of her name on his lips filled her with pleasure, and she rushed from the office before he could see the tears filling her eyes. As the door closed behind her, Verity breathed again, taking in great gulps of air

to calm herself. Her heart was racing and she felt totally
bewildered. It was too late now, thought Verity crossly.
Despite everything, her feelings for Saul were changing.
Verity leaned against her desk for support and closed
her eyes, shaking her head. She had to admit that, like
a silly teenager, she seemed to be falling in love with her
boss, and he was blissfully unaware of it. At least I hope
he is! Verity blushed at the thought of his knowing—
that would just be unbearable. I can't be falling in love
with him, she corrected herself; then she shook her head
sadly. What on earth was she going to do now?

'Miss Chambers,' purred a familiar voice, breaking
into her thoughts and making Verity start, 'Tell Saul I'm
here; we're off to lunch.' Imogen's eyes narrowed as she
spoke. 'There's nothing wrong, is there?'

'No,' snapped Verity, and she turned and called Saul.
He entered the office immediately, and his very presence
dominated the room as usual. Verity busied herself with
some papers, trying hard to concentrate on her work.

'Imogen, I had quite forgotten,' he said apologetically, pulling on his jacket as he spoke.

'Aren't you the naughty one?' she chastised, waving
an admonishing finger at him. Verity grimaced at her
actions, and looked at Saul; he raised his dark brows
with amusement. Then, as Imogen wrapped a possessive
arm through his, they left. Verity watched them leave
and sighed with relief; at least he would be gone for the
rest of the afternoon. I'll have to leave—this situation
is impossible, she decided. Verity felt sick; what on earth
was she going to do? I'll have to make some excuse about
working part-time for Hannah's sake, she thought as
she bit into a tasteless sandwich. Pushing the hair from

her shoulders, she decided she would phone the agency at once.

Yet all her good intentions faded like the dew in the morning once the flowers arrived. Verity stared in disbelief at the huge bouquet of roses and smiled; she read the note once again and her heart leapt for joy. 'Thank you for a lovely time in France.' Verity could hardly wait for Saul to return; she knew this time that he had no ulterior motive. He had genuinely sent the flowers as a 'Thank you' and Verity was delighted.

'Saul!' she cried with pleasure the moment he entered the office. He stopped, looking at Verity's animated face in amazement.

'I see you have had flowers delivered,' he said coolly.

'Yes, I have, and they're lovely, aren't they?' Verity enthused, breathing in their heady perfume. He nodded in agreement and walked straight past into his office. Typical, thought Verity crossly; the only time he does anything remotely human and he doesn't want it acknowledged. She set to work with a happy heart and the time flew by. Suddenly the office door opened and Saul stood there, his eyes like diamond chips. 'There's a call for you on my private line,' he barked. Verity faltered; who on earth could be phoning her? 'Quickly, woman— it's long distance,' he snapped, and Verity darted past him into his office.

She paused before picking up the phone, then she asked cautiously, 'Hello, who is it, please?'

'*Bonjour, ma petite,*' the sexy voice of Étienne drawled in reply.

'Étienne!' cried Verity in surprise. 'How lovely! What a good day I'm having—first the roses, then a call from you.'

'Roses,' he echoed. 'Did you receive the roses? I wanted to deliver them in person, but I could not,' he whispered seductively down the phone.

'Oh, *you* sent them!' Verity replied, disappointed.

'*Mais oui*; do you mean I have a rival for your affections?' he asked, trying to sound injured.

'No, no, not at all; thank you, they're really beautiful.'

'It was my pleasure—a small token for the lovely time we had together. I hope to see you soon, *ma petite*, very soon.' And with that he was gone. Verity replaced the phone thoughtfully, pushing her long hair from her face, and sighed.

'Well, well, well,' mocked the icy tone of Saul as he leaned indolently against the door-jamb, a wry smile on his face.

'Well what?' snapped Verity angrily, taking an instant dislike to his smug expression.

'What did he want?'

'To see if I had received the roses he sent,' replied Verity triumphantly.

'He sent? He told you?' Saul echoed angrily. 'Roses, as a sweetener. Did they work?' he asked drily, his eyes flashing with temper.

'I don't know what you mean,' stated Verity, meeting his gaze head-on in defiance and speaking in a bored tone as she strolled over towards him. As she passed him in the doorway, his arm shot out, effectively blocking her way, and the grim expression on his face made Verity's blood run cold.

'When are you going?' he asked with a distasteful look on his face.

'I have no idea what you're talking about,' Verity replied, trying to keep her composure despite being somewhat alarmed by his sudden change of mood.

'Oh, I see; he hasn't asked you yet,' he continued with droll cynicism.

'Asked me what?' asked Verity, suddenly perturbed. Saul gave a hollow laugh and shook his head.

'You really are an innocent. Why on earth do you think he is sending you flowers?'

'As a "Thank you".'

'He is thanking you in anticipation, believe me,' his deep voice drawled mockingly.

'You disgust me,' retorted Verity as the truth dawned and she realised what he was implying.

'Really? I rather hoped it would be the behaviour of that Don Juan that would disgust you.' His eyes flashed with irritation, but Verity was heedless of his temper.

'Just because you send flowers as a bribe doesn't mean everyone does,' she retorted spitefully. 'Is that what you have to do—send flowers to persuade a woman to sleep with you?' she taunted with biting anger. He stiffened as she spoke, his eyes glittering dangerously, and a cold steel sharpness was in his voice.

'You go too far, Verity,' he warned, his voice quiet but threatening.

'Maybe I should phone the florist now; what is Imogen's address?' she smiled sweetly as she spoke, not caring about the consequences, and she tossed back her head so that her hair fell about her shoulders in soft waves.

'Enough!' roared Saul as his fist came crashing down on the door, and Verity jumped in alarm. His temper was evident in every line on his dangerous, ruthless face.

His eyes burned and Verity moved away, seeing the menace, the threat of violence in his body. Her heart was racing, beating painfully against her breastbone, her pulse tearing along at an uncomfortable rate. Saul stood in front of her, the strain of keeping his self-control visible on his taut face. His hands gripped her shoulders, his long fingers digging deep into her flesh, but Verity was too afraid even to call out.

'Now,' he drawled, his voice tight, 'one more word out of you—just one—' he emphasised '——and you'll find yourself in trouble. Do I make myself clear?'

She stared at him, their eyes locked in a silent battle. She hated him, she knew that now; she hated him more than she had ever thought possible. She nodded, her mouth closed tightly in anger. He smiled, and her blood ran cold.

'Good,' he murmured as he looked down at her angry face. Verity viewed him with barely concealed resentment. She marched past him and as she did so he whacked her hard across her rear. Verity swung round but he raised his hand to silence her. 'Not a word; you deserved that and more,' he warned. He closed the office door behind him; taking the florist's receipt from his pocket, he tore it into little pieces, letting it drop from his hands like confetti. He shook his head. 'You deserve each other,' he mumbled bitterly to himself, yet a part of him felt he should convince Verity of the truth. He sighed; there was no way she would believe him anyway.

Verity dissolved into tears of rage; they flowed in torrents—she was so angry, and filled with a burning bitter resentment. She had never felt so humiliated in all her life. It was good to make Saul feel as angry, though, and

Saul *was* angry. No, he was furious, thought Verity, and grinned as she looked around her office. There were flowers everywhere; the bouquets were being delivered every hour on the hour and there was only one way they would stop being sent—if Verity agreed to go and meet Étienne in Paris. He would be there for the weekend, and hoped she would join him. She had always wanted to see Paris, and Étienne had generously booked her single accommodation at a top-class hotel, as well as arranging the air ticket. It seemed almost churlish to refuse. That night she asked Mrs Collins for her opinion.

'You go, love; me and Hannah will be just fine together,' smiled Mrs Collins.

'I'm not sure... I'd love to go, but...' Verity faltered; she had an uneasy doubt in her mind.

'It's a golden opportunity. You ask your boss and you finish early on Friday, and I'll see to Hannah for the weekend. I want to see that new Disney film myself. Just think—you could be spending two whole days in Paris.'

Verity was torn, though she desperately wanted to see Paris, and even to spend some time with Étienne; but she knew Saul would disapprove. I have to go, she decided. I am only an employee to Saul, it might help me to get him out of my system, she thought.

'Is it OK if I finish early on Friday night?' asked Verity politely as she placed some neatly typed letters on his desk.

'Why?'

'I have to go out. I should like a little extra time to get ready,' Verity replied, but she kept her eyes lowered, unable to face him.

'Where are you going?' he asked in the same cool voice that demanded a full explanation. Verity bristled with anger and a dread that if this conversation continued he might discover her secret.

'Hannah's in a concert at school,' she lied hurriedly, turning to leave; but she paused as he called her name.

'Verity...' He paused and looked at her, a frown creasing his forehead, a suspicious, doubtful look in his eyes. 'Have a good time.'

'Thanks,' mumbled Verity, colouring with embarrassment at her deception.

Now that she was flying off to Paris to meet Étienne, the excitement of the trip pushed all doubts from her mind. He was there on business, and to her it was an ideal time to be shown the city. She would be able to stay at a hotel in the very heart of the city and, as if to allay any of her fears, he had assured her it was a single room. He was such a gentleman, mused Verity, and so thoughtful. She nodded silently to herself; yes, it was an excellent opportunity—it would have been silly to miss it just because of Saul's low opinion of Étienne, which was obviously a result of whatever had happened between them all that time ago. As arranged, Étienne met her at the airport; he strode across to her, smiling warmly, his olive-tanned skin dark against his white shirt and pale-coloured trousers. He was a complete contrast to the sombre Mr Easton, she mused.

'Ma chérie!' he called endearingly, wrapping his arms around her and pulling her close. Verity faltered for a moment then put it down to custom and her own English stuffiness and hugged him warmly back. The drive back into the city was hectic in the rush-hour traffic, but Verity still enjoyed every minute, taking in all the sights with delight. Finally Étienne drew the car up outside an apartment block. It was impressive, to say the least. Verity was puzzled.

'Where are we?' she asked, trying to suffocate the doubts that were beginning to surface at the back of her mind.

'It is terrible, I know, but there was not a decent hotel with a room to spare. Weekends are always busy in Paris. My apartment, *chérie*, is large enough for two, and is far cosier,' he said, a dangerous smile playing on his lips.

'I don't want to put you to any trouble—any hotel would be fine,' Verity said quickly, not wishing to offend Étienne, but she was unsure about his sincerity. He smiled again, his white teeth almost flashing in a predatory fashion.

'If you wish, but at least come and see my humble abode; you can refresh yourself, change for dinner, then if you still wish I shall gladly take you to an 'otel,' he reassured her as he leaned over and took her overnight bag from the rear of the car.

Verity smiled and vowed silently to spend the night in the safety of a hotel room. 'Surely they're not originals?' asked Verity in awe as she stared at the collection of Impressionist paintings that adorned the endless wall.

'Of course. They are not to my taste; but the value is increasing all the time,' he explained excitedly. Verity felt herself bristle at his obvious delight in their monetary value instead of their worth as works of art.

'I have booked us a meal at Le Bonnard; you will enjoy the beautiful food, and the views of Paris are breathtaking.' He smiled warmly, his eyes betraying a hunger she had not noticed before. Verity felt herself colour and she tried to cover her embarrassment. Étienne sat down beside her, taking her hand gently in his and stroking it.

'I've longed to see you,' he murmured closely in her ear. Verity stiffened and swallowed hard.

'It's very kind of you to invite me; I can't think how I'm ever going to repay you,' Verity said as she tried to move a little away from him.

'I'm sure you will more than repay my generosity,' he answered, as he leaned even closer, a glint of desire in his eyes.

Verity put on her most efficient, icy tone. 'I hope this is going to be a pleasant weekend, Étienne; I certainly wouldn't have come if——'

'If what, *ma petite*? Relax, we shall enjoy ourselves— but naturally I was hoping that we would become more than friends,' he said persuasively, and his youthful face looked so full of hopeful expectation that Verity felt she couldn't deny.

'I think we should take things slowly, Étienne; we hardly know each other,' suggested Verity.

'I have something that will help you relax,' he smiled.

Verity watched him leave the room, a chill of realisation that Saul might have been right about Étienne beginning to take root inside her. He reappeared within moments with a chilled bottle of Don Pérignon. Verity's eyebrows rose in surprise.

'That's terribly expensive,' she said, eyeing the bottle.

'*Oui*, but one has to pay for the best things in life, and I'm sure you're worth it.' Verity gave a half-smile as he opened the bottle and poured two glasses. As he passed her one he said, 'To us, and an unforgettable weekend in Paris,' and he kissed her lightly on the cheek.

'To Paris,' answered Verity, lowering her eyes.

'You wish to change for dinner, no? So use this bedroom; there is a bathroom en suite,' he added as he escorted Verity to the door. She smiled sweetly and shut the door firmly. Placing her overnight case on the bed, she began to unpack, her uneasy feeling growing. Verity dressed with care; she had brought a new dress, and knew this was the occasion to wear it. The cool ivory silk shift hung over her lissom body, accentuating her female curves. The row of pearl buttons that fastened the front glistened, adding a glow to the already shimmering fabric. Verity coiled her hair around two beautiful mother-of-pearl combs, and the finished result was stunning.

'You are beautiful—like a goddess.' Étienne's eyes travelled over her body, taking in every detail, and she felt herself colour as his seductive eyes met hers.

'Shall we go?' she said brightly, trying to sound confident and friendly.

'I don't know whether I want to go out now; why should I share you with others?' he said, pulling her gently on to the soft leather couch. Verity stiffened, and her breathing became more rapid as she thought frantically of something to say.

'Now come on—I'm starving,' she said as firmly as she could, easing herself away from him. It was then that she noticed the empty bottle and felt the firm grip he had taken of her arm.

'I'm starving too,' he said lecherously as he licked his thick lips and moved closer. Verity tried to move, but he pinned her down firmly against the couch, his own breathing heavy and his hands holding her head. She felt his wet lips on hers, hard and demanding. She tried to pull her head away, but his onslaught was relentless. She struggled weakly beneath him, her hands pulling at his hair, his back, anywhere she could take a hold and perhaps hurt him. His hands had began to explore her body in a crude, emotionless way. His hands pulled clumsily at her dress till the buttons fell away, scattering over the floor. His fingers were seeking and greedy, and Verity cringed at his touch. She felt exposed, and, fighting with all her might, she managed to break free.

'Why have you gone suddenly cold, or do you just prefer this way?' He swayed drunkenly towards her, the stench of alcohol on his breath. He grabbed her, and they fell together on to the floor. Verity felt his knee trying to force her thighs apart and sheer panic gave her a new charge of strength. She drew her knee up and rammed it against him. He groaned loudly and fell back, holding himself as he rocked on the floor. Verity ran, sobbing, pulling her torn dress across her body. She ran from the building as if the devil himself were after her. She heard a Frenchman call something to her, but she wasn't listening—she just ran till finally the pain in her side forced her to stop. Panting hard, she looked at herself; she fastened up what buttons still existed and tried to straighten her hair. She had nothing—no money, no clothes, not even her passport. Verity was in trouble, and she only knew one person she could turn to.

It was with a heavy heart that Verity entered a nearby hotel. She looked around quickly, aware of many patrons giving her strange looks. Undeterred, she made her way to the phone kiosk, and the operator told her that her caller would accept the reverse charge. The moment Verity heard Saul's familiar voice she began to weep.

'Verity? Verity; is that you?' he called anxiously.

'Yes—oh, Saul, Saul!' she sobbed down the phone, in danger of becoming hysterical.

'What on earth are you doing there?' he asked, puzzled.

'Étienne invit——' she began.

'Étienne?' he spat, then he sighed. 'The name,' he snapped. 'Just give me the name of the hotel and stay put,' he ordered.

'Metropole.'

'Metropole—you're sure?'

'Yes,' she stammered in reply, then the phone went dead. Within moments a bemused-looking receptionist tapped politely on the side of the kiosk.

'*Excusez-moi*, you are Verity Chambers, *oui*?'

'*Oui.*' was the monosyllabic reply Verity gave. The receptionist guided Verity through the foyer and up in the lift to a suite of rooms. Verity's puzzled look was soon replaced with one of relief as the girl explained that Mr Easton had telephoned them to arrange accommodation. Verity sat down on the huge bed, her mind in a turmoil. She felt dirty, used, and very stupid. She went into the bathroom and stood under the shower, rubbing and scrubbing away at her body to remove any trace of Étienne.

She had no idea how long she stood there—everything seemed so unreal, like a terrible nightmare, and Verity shuddered when she thought of Saul. The inevitable confrontation with him was not something she was looking forward to. If she had only listened to him this would not have happened, and Verity began to cry again. After showering, Verity wrapped herself in a huge soft peach bath sheet, tied up a second towel around her head, and lay down on the bed. She fell into a restless sleep; her dreams were tormented with images of Étienne, and then Saul's face would become superimposed. Verity cried out and awoke with a start.

'You're all right, relax, everything is fine,' said a calm, reassuring voice, and she felt someone patting her leg reassuringly.

'Saul, Saul, is that you?' asked Verity, immediately alert.

'Yes; you were sleeping when I arrived so I just sat here and waited.' His voice sounded wonderfully warm and strong, and Verity gave a sigh of relief. He snapped the lamp on at the side of the bed and Verity closed her eyes, afraid to look at him. She began to tremble, suddenly aware of her lack of clothing.

'Have you eaten?' he asked abruptly, picking up the phone.

'No—we didn't go out to dinner,' she replied, and tears pricked at her eyes as she recalled what had happened. Saul ordered for both of them, and within moments a tray of sandwiches and a pot of steaming coffee arrived. He poured the coffee and offered it to her. She drank some, the hot liquid warming her and bringing her back to her senses. She kept her eyes lowered, her long lashes flickering against her white face. She felt him watching her and risked a quick glance at him through her lashes. He was pale too, his eyes were grim, and his face had an austere expression that frightened her. He idly picked up a sandwich and paced to the window looking out across the city, his back to her.

'I warned you—I knew something like this would happen.' His voice was quiet, thoughtful, but there was an underlying anger that Verity knew he was trying to control. She said nothing; any words seemed rather futile, pointless.

'Tell me, is there any need to inform the police?' His voice was icy, and Verity was puzzled by the question.

'The police?' she echoed, looking at Saul, and watching him stiffen as he awaited the reply.

He swung round to face her, his dark eyes glittering brilliantly; he surveyed her trembling body, the puzzled look on her tear-stained face. He sighed audibly and snapped, 'Damn you, Verity, did he rape you?' he almost shouted, his fists clenched at his side so tightly that his knuckles were white. Verity gasped and lowered her head, shaking it negatively as she did so. Saul's clenched fist thundered down on the tray, almost knocking it from the bed. Verity's head shot up, the towel falling from her head, and her damp hair cascaded over her bare shoulders.

'No, he didn't,' she said emphatically. 'He was drunk and he started to——' She stopped, unable to carry on as she began to cry. Saul placed the tray on the floor and sat on the bed; wrapping his arms around her, he cradled her tightly as he rocked her gently to and fro.

'Hush, now, it's all over; shush, rest now,' he whispered softly in her ear. Slowly, comforted by his reassuring voice and his strong hand gently smoothing her wet hair from her face, Verity stopped crying. She leaned against his hard chest, secure in his arms.

'I'm sorry,' she mumbled, unable to think of anything else to say.

Loosening his hold on her, he mumured, 'It's OK. Everything will be all right.' She raised her head to look at him, and she heard him take a sharp intake of breath. 'Verity, you don't know how much I've wanted you!' His mouth sought and found hers. At first Verity struggled, the memory of Étienne still fresh in her mind.

She tried to force Saul away, but the weight of his body was too heavy and after a while the feel of his strong, hard body against hers seduced her into a state of exquisite delight. She felt herself sinking into a sea of desire, responding to his touch despite herself.

'Saul,' she moaned, 'please, Saul!' But her voice was unheeded as they drew closer, their mouths seeking one another. He buried his face in her damp hair.

'I warned you,' he muttered violently, 'but you continue to taunt me. You must have known how much I wanted you.' His mouth was on hers again, his kisses slow but forceful. Verity weakened as her body responded, moulding itself against his. The towel fell from her body and she heard him mumble a curse before he descended upon her soft breasts. He cupped them gently in his hand, stroking his thumb across her nipples till they grew taut and erect, then his hot lips began to kiss them, his tongue tracing the aureoles with a slow deliberation. Verity moaned softly; she didn't want to struggle any more. She raised her arms up, wrapped them around his neck, and drew him down upon her. She wanted to give herself completely to him. His hands stroked the length of her body while his lips still devoured her, arousing Verity till nothing else mattered. Then he stopped and drew back so abruptly that Verity felt chilled. He gave a muffled cry of self-disgust as he stood, running his tapered fingers through his raven-black hair. Verity gazed up at him, the hurt and bewilderment in her eyes.

'Cover yourself, Verity,' he snapped, his back still turned towards her.

'Saul,' she began earnestly, 'I wanted to——'

'Don't let's even talk about it,' he growled, turning to face her, his eyes troubled. 'I'm sorry for what has just happened. I know an apology isn't worth much after what you have been through tonight. I really am sorry to have taken advantage of the situation,' he said coldly, his eyes ice-blue.

'Saul, you're wrong—I'm not a child.'

'For God's sake, Verity, does it look as if I think you're a child?' he thundered.

'No,' she began uneasily, 'but you don't seem to credit me with any intelligence. I knew full well what I was doing, and I wanted to. Don't you understand, Saul? I wanted to.' She was shouting now, her eyes bright with passion.

'Yes, I understand, Verity; I understand more than you think,' he snapped back, his eyes like diamond chips as he looked at her angry upturned face.

'What do you mean?' she asked, a cold chill running the length of her back. He sighed audibly and ran his fingers through his tousled hair in a familiar gesture of temper.

'You have woken up at last, realised you're alive with feelings; you're a woman with a woman's needs, but to-morrow, Verity, in the cold light of day——'

'Tomorrow?' she interrupted angrily. 'Let's not think of that now.'

'I have to; damn you, Verity, I have to!' And he strode from the room, the door slamming with finality. Verity took several deep breaths, then felt the hot tears squeeze their way out of her lids, flowing in a soft unending river down her pale face. She cried in total silence, not daring to make a sound in case he heard her. She sank her white teeth into her bottom lip, biting it, and she closed her eyes tightly, screwing them up to shut out the reality. She sat on the bed, staring ahead, her face a blank sheet, her mind empty. Slowly the tears ceased but still she didn't move.

She just sat there, for a long, long time. She was numb, unable to think, unable to move, just sitting, trying to compose herself. The incident had been devastating. He had knocked down every barrier she had ever erected. She had to admit it—she was powerfully attracted to him, and yet he had been right. How was she to face him tomorrow? She rubbed her hands across her face and shuddered. Saul had come crashing through her stone wall in one fell swoop. He had slowly been eroding her defences, stirring her back to life despite her reluctance; but tonight had been different. He had crashed down the walls with such intensity that she had been unable to cope. The electricity between them shattered all her preconceptions of him. She knew now that they were a dangerous combination. She must never let him near her again. There was a powerful attraction between them that she knew would be impossible to control. Yet what was even worse was the fact that Saul didn't love her. He wanted her; those were his exact words—'I've wanted you.' But that wasn't love, and Verity knew with a heaviness of heart that that was what *she* wanted.

CHAPTER SEVEN

'ARE you awake, Verity?' called Saul as he rapped on the door.

Verity grimaced. Of course I'm awake—I've hardly slept all night, she wanted to scream. She coloured as she recalled last night's events and her total humiliation.

'Verity? Verity?' His voice was loud and insistent; he was almost shouting. Verity looked round, frantically looking for something to wear; the knocking continued, increasing in volume. He was obviously in a temper. She stumbled to the door, wrapping a sheet around her body. She opened it with one hand while clutching the sheet with the other.

'I would have thought it a little late for modesty,' he growled, his dark eyes flickering over her attire with cynicism. Verity coloured and lowered her head, casting a swift glance at his face; it was starkly set, austere and forbidding. He strode past her and desposited her case on the floor.

'Your things,' he snapped, without looking at her.

'How on earth——?' began Verity, pleased that she now had something to wear.

'I went round for them,' Saul stated coldly, answering her question before she had time to finish.

'Oh, I see; thanks.' She wanted to say more, to ask what had been said, but the austere look on Saul's face prevented her doing so. He was angry, a cold furious anger that frightened Verity.

125

'I'll see you at breakfast; don't be long,' he ordered, before marching from the room. Verity stood under the shower for as long as she dared; the thought of facing Saul was tightening her stomach into knots. It was all so difficult, she mused, and embarrassing. She chose her clothes with care; she wanted to give him no indication that she was trying to attract him in any way.

Finally, dressed in a pair of navy trousers and a crisp pale blue blouse, she went downstairs to the dining-room. It was a large, bright, airy room, with high ceilings from which hung two beautiful glass chandeliers. Saul was sitting by an open window, dressed in lightweight casual clothes. Verity's heart thudded the moment she saw him. He was gazing out on to the busy street. His look was distant, his mind far-away, though his eyes looked troubled. Not wishing to disturb him, Verity slipped into the chair opposite him unnoticed. She tried not to look at him, yet she felt his cold eyes staring at her. Whenever she looked at him she was unable to hold his gaze; his eyes pierced her very being. The memories of last night flooded back and she blushed hotly. The silence that hung between them over breakfast was almost tangible but Verity dared not to speak; she bit at her lip and stared down at the fresh rolls in front of her, wishing she had never come to Paris.

'What do you think of Paris?' he suddenly asked.

'Unfortunately, I only saw a little on the drive back from the airport,' confessed Verity, keeping her head down.

'Have you any desire to stay here?' he asked, as if aware of her thoughts.

'No, none. I think it's best I go back home.' She kept her head lowered, her voice low.

'Is that going to be a permanent affliction?' he taunted.

'What do you mean?' she replied, still not facing him.

'The quiet voice, the lowered head—it's not you,' he mocked. Verity raised her head slowly and looked directly into his eyes, willing them to stay fixed. 'Verity, last night...' he began.

'Forget it, I don't want to talk about it.' There was a tremor in her voice as she spoke and she could feel the tears pricking like a thousand pin-heads at the back of her eyes.

'Damn, you, Verity, *I* want to talk about it!' he growled, stretching across the table and gripping her wrist. Verity flinched and the pain was reflected for a second in his eyes. Then she noticed for the first time that he looked tired, drained; his eyes had dark shadows beneath them, and Verity felt sure there was a bluish mark near his left eye.

'I'm sorry about last night, truly I am. It was unforgivable of me. I haven't any excuse except I was acting on instinct; had you not been so——'

'Available?' she snapped; she could hear the excuse in his voice, and bristled.

'That's not true; you know what I mean!'

'What do you mean?' she retorted furiously. 'Had I not been? Had I not been what? You say there was no excuse, and then blame me.'

'I'm not blaming anyone; it just shouldn't have happened.' He shifted restlessly in his chair, uncomfortable with the way the conversation was going.

'Why shouldn't it have happened—we both wanted to, didn't we?' she asked, desperate for his reassurance, longing for him to admit to feeling something for her.

He sighed. 'Look, let's leave it, shall we? I'm sorry, but I'm only human.'

'That's quite an admission for you; I always regarded you as a machine—relentless and hard.' She felt bitter now; she didn't want his apology, she wanted him. Did he not understand that? His eyes had darkened to ebony, flashing lights danced in them, and he looked at her grimly.

'I think I proved last night beyond any doubt that I am fully human,' he sneered, enjoying the colour that rushed to her cheeks. 'I quite understand if you feel working for me would be impossible now,' he added, looking directly at her. Verity smiled, a bubbling anger inside her.

'Mr Easton, if you are unhappy with the standard of my work, say so—don't look for excuses.' She was determined to make this difficult for him.

'I thought perhaps you would find it difficult now——' he began to explain.

'Mr Easton, I too am sorry for what happened last night. My only excuss is that I must have been a little drunk, but rest assured a similiar incident will never arise again,' she stated emphatically, then added, 'Maybe I should have stayed with Étienne.'

She heard the harsh intake of breath, saw Saul's lean body stiffen, but he didn't try to answer her, although the table shook with his angry emotion. She had tried to goad him, to force the words from him, but he just sat, his eyes glittering as he stared at her. She stood, and walked quickly back up to her room, where she lay on the bed and cried.

'We shall be leaving at two p.m.,' announced Saul as he poked his head around the door; if he noticed Verity's distress he made no comment about it.

After that they didn't speak again, which made the journey home seem long and tiring. Verity constantly tried to make some sense out of the incident but her own emotions were too volatile to reason. She pretended to read the novel she had brought but the words blurred in front of her eyes. She raised her eyes, keeping her head lowered, and glanced up at Saul. He sat pale and stony-faced, his chiselled features looked hard and un- relenting, and his eyes smouldered with annoyance.

Verity was determined to be as cool as Saul. There was no future with him, and she wasn't even sure she wanted one with him anyway. He was cold and hard, obviously incapable of loving anyone—no wonder his first wife left him, Verity thought as they travelled back, yet there was a niggling doubt in the back of her mind that she refused fully to acknowledge.

The return to work on Monday saw Saul in no better humour, and it improved little, if at all, over the ensuing weeks. The contempt and fury he had treated her with since their return was almost unbearable. Verity re- turned to her former self, betraying no emotion but re- maining calm regardless of the provocation. Thankfully the workload was hectic, which acted as a welcome panacea, and, as Saul was working on a new deal, they rarely saw one another...

'Verity, isn't it?' smiled Imogen, interrupting Verity as she searched frantically through her files looking for a lost letter of importance.

'Yes,' she answered distractedly. 'I'm sorry, but Saul isn't in. Do you want to leave a message?'

'Well, actually, darling, I came to see you. You see, I've heard a little rumour.' She gave a brittle laugh as she spoke. 'I'm sure it's silly nonsense.'

'What is it?' snapped Verity, disliking the interruption, and bewildered as to what it could be that would involve her...

'A little bird told me that you and Saul took off to Paris for the weekend. It's probably nonsense.'

'If you believe it's nonsense, I fail to see why you came to ask me about it,' retorted Verity sharply.

'Well, you're hardly his type. I know I shouldn't listen to gossip but, well, I do tend to be a little green-eyed where he is concerned; you understand, don't you?' she purred, trying to sound friendly although her smile never reached her eyes.

'Yes, we did go to Paris.' Verity delighted in the stunned look on Imogen's face.

'I don't believe you. What on earth would he see in a person like you?' the blonde woman sneered, waving a perfectly manicured hand dismissively at her. Verity bristled, though what Imogen had said was undoubtedly true.

'If you don't believe it, then I don't see why you have come here to ask me,' repeated Verity triumphantly, enjoying Imogen's discomfort.

'He's mine!' she spat, her eyes gleaming with jealousy.

'I don't think he belongs to anyone,' Verity snapped back, unaware that Saul had entered the office and was viewing the two women in disbelief.

'Imogen, what a delight to see you,' he declared, his radiant smile bringing a brightness to the room. She turned and ran towards him, flinging her arms around his neck in a possessive gesture.

'Darling, you simply must come to dinner at my place tonight—just the two of us,' she said in a simpering voice quite unlike the strident, discordant screech that Verity had had to listen to.

'I'll be delighted—about eight-thirty?'

'Super, and I shall cook it all myself, just for you.' She pouted as she spoke, then, smiling triumphantly at Verity, she wafted out of the room. Verity watched with an amused grin on her face. If anyone was going to have him it would be Imogen, she thought, and she then felt a stab of resentment.

Saul looked at Verity, his dark eyes warning her of his wrath. 'My office, now,' he barked, obviously annoyed by her amusement.

'I have to find——'

'Now!' His icy tone brooked no argument, and Verity stiffened. She wondered whether or not she had given him the excuse to fire her. Verity was confused; she was no longer very happy in her work, but the thought of never seeing Saul again was even worse.

She walked into his office with deliberate composure. He was looking out of the window, his hands pushed deep into his pockets; his very stance was arrogant and self-assured. He turned abruptly to face Verity.

'What was all that about?' he growled, pacing as he spoke.

'You heard most of it, didn't you?' she retorted, caring little about what he thought.

'I heard you informing Imogen that we had spent a weekend in Paris,' he stated, his dark eyes flashing with flames of anger. Verity half smiled at the memory of Imogen's shocked expression, but she soon stopped as Saul's face grew sterner. 'We did not go to Paris together, *you* went to Paris. I merely rescued you after you made a fool of yourself.'

'For which I am eternally grateful,' she answered sarcastically. Saul grew white with anger, his eyes darkening to ebony.

'What's that supposed to mean?' he growled.

'Exactly that; I learned a lot in Paris, and I shall always be grateful to you,' she explained, blazing with anger. He grabbed at her wrist, pulling her towards him; she fell against him and her head fell back.

'Nothing happened in Paris; you would do well to remember that, and certainly,' he emphasised, 'don't pretend to anyone else that something happened—but most importantly, Verity, don't fool yourself.'

The last biting remark really hurt, and Verity's eyes filled immediately. She swallowed and took a steadying breath.

'Verity, I——' He stopped. Whatever he was going to say would have been wasted, as Verity had already left the room.

She sat down heavily, her head between her hands. She had no idea how long she sat there; she was too numb to care.

'Are you Miss Verity Chambers?' an icy voice asked, and Verity raised her head. Two large almond-shaped eyes bored into her. They were icy-grey like flint, and just as hard. The woman was tall, very tall, so chic, so elegant that every item of clothing screamed wealth. She had blonde hair that had been so professionally highlighted that it looked natural. The perfume she was wearing hung in the air, its aroma sexy and overpowering.

'Yes.' Verity smiled politely, but the warmth of her smile was not returned.

'Then this trash belongs to you.' With that the woman emptied a plastic bag of toiletries over Verity's desk, her contempt and disdain apparent in every movement. Verity gasped in horror as the toiletries spilt, some clattering to the floor. 'You little whore!' she spat, the hatred glittering in her eyes. Verity was stunned; she had no idea who this woman was, but her dislike of Verity was clear enough.

'Please—I'm very sorry...' began Verity frantically, her heart racing, but the woman's eyes narrowed even further and the anger she felt for Verity was evident.

'*Sorry? Sorry?* You don't know the meaning of the word!' She glared at Verity as she spoke. Then, with a sudden, swift movement, she slapped Verity hard across her face, dragging her long nails down her cheek with deliberation. She raised her hand to slap her again, but Saul's chilling voice froze her hand in mid-flight.

'What on earth...?' he began, then his eyes narrowed as he saw the woman. 'Long time no see,' he drawled, his eyes flickering over the woman's body appreciatively. The colour drained from her face; the voice had been instantly recognised. She turned slowly, her eyes widening in disbelief. They stood facing each other, the tension and mutual dislike filled the space between them. They eyed each other warily, each making an appraisal of the other. The woman opened her mouth as if she was about to speak, but Saul had gripped her by the hand and was propelling her into his office, a cold look of fury on his face.

Verity rubbed her cheek distractedly, her mind firmly focused on Saul and that woman. She could hear the woman's voice loud and strident, with a faint accent. Then, equally loud but with a biting edge, Verity would hear the rumblings of Saul's voice, but there were no distinguishable words. Verity tried to carry on with her work, but she found it impossible.

The door suddenly swung open and the pair of them came from the office. They stopped in front of Verity and the woman, still viewing Verity, said with disdain, 'I think perhaps I owe you an apology.'

'You certainly do!' barked Saul.

The apology was mumbled and before Verity could reply the woman had swept out of the office, leaving the same expensive perfume lingering in the air.

'Turn on the air-conditioning; let's get rid of that stench,' Saul growled before turning on his heel and marching back into the office. The door slammed, its reverberations echoing across the offices. Verity got up immediately and followed him, determined to find out who the woman was.

'Yes?' said Saul in a bored tone, not troubling himself to raise his head. Verity looked down at him, noticing the way the late afternoon sunlight softened the outline of his face.

'I want to know who that female was,' she said calmly, her voice not betraying the turmoil she felt inside.

'Do you?' he answered, his head still bent on his work. Verity waited, but he said no more.

'Yes, I do,' Verity persisted.

He looked up suddenly, and his dark eyes fixed upon her with an intensity that bored into her very being. Yet his expression was unfathomable. The silence was tangible, ominous and disturbing. Verity held his gaze with equal candour, though her heart was racing and her mind a bubbling cauldron of questions.

'That was Madame Bouvier...' He paused, then said, knowing the impact his words would make, 'Étienne's wife.' A half-smile played on his lips; he was pleased that his words had stunned Verity. She gave a quiet gasp of surprise, her eyes widening in disbelief. She shifted uncomfortably then nodded silently.

'You can understand her reaction to you now, I presume?' he sneered, his face grim.

'Yes,' began Verity, then she faltered, 'but I thought, he did say...' Her face burned with colour.

'And you believed him?' Saul shook his head mockingly and gave a cruel laugh.

'Yes,' admitted Verity reluctantly, 'I did; anyway, we were just friends,' she excused. Saul's eyebrows rose in surprise. 'Hardly friends—a weekend in Paris, at his apartment,' he jeered.

Verity stiffened. 'It wasn't like that,' she insisted, her eyes flashing, and she flicked the hair back from her shoulders in annoyance.

'Really?' There was an unspoken anger in his voice that was just discernible, and his eyes had narrowed to diamond chips as he watched her intently.

'Yes, you know damn well what happened!' she shouted indignantly.

'Please don't raise your voice to me; there is no need,' he replied with such composure that Verity had to fight the desire to strike him.

'There obviously is a need, or I wouldn't have to do it. You know full well what happened that weekend,' Verity stormed, her face flushed, her eyes shining with a glittering brilliance.

'Do I? I only know what you told me,' he retorted. The implication was too much for Verity. She felt her anger go suddenly to be replaced with a cold self-righteousness. 'I told you the truth,' she stated simply.

'The whole truth?' he snapped back, as he ran his fingers through his hair, pushing it back from his harsh face.

'What do you mean by that?' she retorted.

'Étienne seems to think you were more than willing.'

Verity swallowed and a flush of colour brightened her face.

'That's a lie.'

Saul gave a sardonic smile and shrugged his powerful shoulders. 'Is it, Verity?' he asked. Verity stiffened; she couldn't believe her ears.

'You know it is. Why are you saying these things?' she questioned, hurt by his attitude; a million sharp pinheads pricked at the back of her eyes. She looked at him, and her bright sapphire eyes, soft with the sorrow of unshed tears, proclaimed her innocence.

'Étienne seems to have convinced his wife he was not entirely to blame,' he explained gruffly, offering her an immaculate silk hankerchief. Verity shook her head in refusal.

'Here, take it,' he snapped, thrusting it at her, and as he did so his hand touched hers and a volt of electricity soared through her. She pulled back instantly, lowering her face to mask her expression. 'I have to know, Verity,' he stated.

'Do you? Why? You seem more than ready to accept his version of what happened. All men together—I was asking for it, no doubt. Does that exonerate your behaviour as well, Saul?' The words spilled out from Verity; she was hurt and bewildered. Saul stood abruptly, his eyes dark and forbidding.

'Don't put words into my mouth, Verity,' he said coldly.

'You accused me——'

'I have accused you of nothing. I just had to be sure.'

'She must have really bowled you over, managing to persuade you I was the villain of the piece. An old flame of yours, was she?' jeered Verity, glaring at him with barely concealed contempt.

'You could say that . . .' He paused quite deliberately before saying, 'She was my wife.'

Verity stared at him in disbelief, gripping the edge of the table for support.

'Your *wife*?' she gasped. He nodded by way of reply, then turned his back and walked over to the window, where he stood staring out across the city. He sank his hands into his trouser pockets; he was deep in thought, and the silence lasted an eternity. Verity was stunned.

'I guess you can understand why the Bouvier deal was so important to me now,' he said, his back still towards her. 'I wanted revenge on Étienne,' he stated simply.

'But why?' asked Verity, shocked by his admission. He turned suddenly, his eyes fiercely bright.

'Amanda wanted the Bouvier château and vineyard, and now Étienne no longer has it. I have.' There was an angry bitterness in the way he spoke and his face looked harsh, his expression almost cruel. Verity shuddered as she looked at him, though she wasn't afraid of him— no, it was more pity he aroused in her. She left his office silently as he sank into his chair and began to work again.

Saul left the office early. 'I'm dining with Imogen tonight,' he said abruptly as he left.

'Enjoy yourself,' answered Verity, her eyes still on her work, her fingers racing furiously over the keys.

'Pardon?' he asked as he covered the keyboard with his fingers. Verity froze, aware of the closeness of his body, the scent of his masculine aftershave filling her nostrils.

'I said enjoy yourself,' she answered.

'Why is it, Verity, that I get the distinct impression you don't really mean that?' he queried, his eyebrows lifted slightly and a glimmer of amusement in his eyes.

'Of course I mean it,' she snapped back. 'Why shouldn't I?'

'I've no idea why; perhaps you would prefer it if I were taking you to dinner?' he mocked, but his expression was quite serious and his dark eyes were fixed on her as he spoke.

Verity felt herself colour, so she kept her head lowered and refused to answer. He waited for a moment, then left. Verity gave a sigh of relief, but her mind was racing. Since coming back from Paris her emotions towards him had swung like a pendulum from anger to pity, from love to hate.

The next day, Verity arrived at the office before Saul, which was unusual, and he still had not appeared at eleven o'clock. Verity had postponed two appointments already and she had tried in vain to reach him at home. She was growing increasingly angry as it was she who had to bear the brunt of the disgruntled businessmen who called. The phone rang and Verity snatched it up, hoping that Saul was finally getting in touch.

'Hello...' There was a pause before a vaguely familiar voice asked, 'Is that you, Verity? It's Mr Ellis.'

'Good morning, Mr Ellis. I'm sorry, but Saul hasn't arrived in yet,' she informed him brightly.

'Not in?' he repeated. 'But there's no answer at his home. I've been trying since late last night.'

'Is there something wrong?' asked Verity, suddenly anxious.

'Yes, it's Heloise; she is ill, very ill, and she wants Saul. Damn him, where is he?' said Mr Ellis, the despair in his voice apparent.

'It's all right; I'll find him, and I'll get him to ring you immediately.'

'Thank you—as quick as you can, now.' The phone went dead and Verity knew exactly where Saul was. The thought incensed her. She flicked quickly through Saul's personal directory; it was an emergency, and she felt sure he wouldn't mind. Then she rapidly dialled Imogen's number.

'Hi,' a warm, lazy voice purred down the phone.

'Good morning, is Mr Easton there?' Verity asked with cool efficiency.

'Saul? Why yes, he is,' Imogen drawled.

'Then can I speak to him, please?'

'It's his hard-working secretary, isn't it?' She laughed shrilly as if she had made some sort of joke.

'Yes, that's right, and it's imperative I speak to Saul now,' Verity snapped.

'I'm ever so sorry but he is still in bed; we both were.' She giggled again and Verity felt a bubbling anger growing.

'Please tell him to telephone me immediately; it's important.'

'Well, we all have our priorities, dear, but work is not everything,' she said pointedly before replacing the receiver.

Verity was furious; she glared at the telephone as she sat and waited for him to return her call. After fifteen minutes she rang Imogen again; the thought of poor little Heloise crying for Saul was incentive enough.

'Hello,' she snapped. 'Can I speak to Saul?'

'Aren't we efficient? Listen, darling, just give me the message and I'll let Saul know,' Imogen said huskily.

'Oh, all right, then.' Verity was too exasperated to argue. 'Tell him Mr Ellis has phoned; Heloise is ill and asking for him.'

'Heloise?' repeated Imogen, her voice suddenly cooler.

'Yes, that's right—Heloise.'

'All right, I'll let him know—but we are occupied at the moment,' she added.

The taxi screeched to a halt outside the mews block of houses. Verity got out hurriedly, thrusting the payment at the driver. 'Keep the change,' she called as she dashed towards the building. He nodded in thanks and drove away.

'Number twenty-three,' said Verity, scanning the doors quickly. She pressed the bell again and again, not pausing in between. She was furious, really furious. She could not comprehend how anyone could treat a child in such a way—especially a sick child.

'You!' gasped Imogen as she opened the door. She was dressed in a very brief silky nightshirt, opened at the top, her firm breasts just becoming visible.

'Where is he?' demanded Verity, pushing right past Imogen and marching into the house. A quick glance round the small lounge and even smaller kitchen confirmed her worst fears.

'He is still in bed, resting,' explained Imogen. 'He spent the night,' she added triumphantly.

'Really? How fascinating,' remarked Verity sarcastically.

'You can't see him, he's . . .' Imogen faltered ' . . . he's ill.'

'He was fine yesterday,' retorted Verity, determined to see Saul.

'I know, and he was all right last night, then shortly after dinner he felt ill,' Imogen said tartly.

'You mean sick.' She couldn't resist the mockery. Imogen flushed.

'What do you mean?' she demanded crossly, viewing Verity with disdain.

'What did you make for dinner?' asked Verity, suddenly concerned.

'I'm an excellent cook,' insisted Imogen. 'I made lobster thermidor,' she said smugly.

'Then I suggest it wasn't fresh—at least Saul's wasn't.'

'Well, I doubt very much it was anything to do with my cooking, and he seemed only too willing to spend the night,' Imogen purred.

'How is he now?' asked Verity frostily, trying to ignore Imogen's obvious remark.

'He is resting; you can't possibly see him now——' she began, but Verity had already run up the stairs, with Imogen in hot pursuit.

'I really think you're going a bit too far,' she spat venomously as she tried to keep pace with Verity.

'Verity?' Saul sat up in surprise as she burst through the door. The covers had fallen from his body as he sat up. He was lean, his chest hard and muscular with a mat of dark hairs. The nakedness of his body emphasised the animal masculinity of the man, and Verity felt her own body respond—a betrayal that annoyed her, though she couldn't help but think what it would be like to run her fingers through those dark curls. His body was glistening with beads of sweat, giving his skin a warm glow. It was more than obvious what kind of exertion he had been up to. Verity flushed as the thought raced through her mind.

'Verity!' called Saul, drawing her away from her own thoughts. She was startled for a moment, then her anger resurged.

'Do you care about anyone but yourself?' she spat, her bright sapphire eyes shining with untold anger.

'What's all this about?' queried Saul, his eyes darting from Imogen to Verity in disbelief.

'How many more times do you want telling?' she yelled, unaware of the surprised look on his face.

'Calm down, Verity, I——' he began, leaning forward in an attempt to touch her.

'Don't you dare lay a finger on me!' she snapped, standing back.

'I wasn't going to; I just want——'

'Want, want—is that all you think about—what *you* want, *your* needs?'

'Verity,' he snapped sternly, a chilling edge to his voice; but it went unheeded. Verity was tired of his cavalier attitude.

'It's bad enough that I have to re-schedule appointments, listen to irate businessmen complaining about your lack of commitment, but when an emergency like this arises and you prefer to stay in bed——'

'I haven't been well; I was going to phone in later. Surely you could cope with any emergency?' he countered, his dark eyes fixed on hers.

'Normally, yes, but what am I supposed to do? It's personal.'

'There's an emergency—personal? What?' he asked anxiously. Verity faltered for a moment, then she turned her blazing eyes on Imogen.

'You haven't told him! You haven't told him, have you?' she accused, her voice tight with anger. Imogen froze and smiled weakly at Saul.

'Darling, I knew you were in no fit state...' she whispered, wrapping her arms around his neck. He shrugged them off and glared at her.

'What's going on?' he demanded, his voice cold with fury.

'I have been trying to reach you all morning; finally I gave Imogen the message to pass on,' Verity explained, relieved, in a sense, that he had not received the message.

'Message, what message?' he demanded, his eyes fixed on Verity.

'I'm sorry, Saul, it's not good...' She paused and swallowed. 'It's Heloise; she is ill, and wants you,' Verity said simply. Then she watched as the little colour he had drained from his face. He leapt up, thrusting the sheets aside, and jumped from the bed with animal agility; then he groaned softly as a wave of nausea swept over him.

'What's wrong with her?' he asked.

'I honestly don't know. Mr Ellis has been trying to reach you since last night,' she explained softly.

'Last night?' he echoed. 'Oh, my God,' he moaned, and sank back on the bed, closing his eyes in an attempt to shut out the reality.

CHAPTER EIGHT

SAUL sank his head wearily into his hands; the shock was too much and he felt too numb to do anything. Verity knew exactly how he was feeling—it was essential that she took control. She braced herself; Saul might see his show of emotion as weakness, but Verity certainly didn't. She looked at him, longing to take him in her arms and to comfort him; but she dismissed such an idea.

'She wants you; are you going?' Verity asked, forcing him to think, to make a decision.

'Of course; do you need to ask?'

'No,' she replied honestly, fixing her sapphire eyes on him. 'I've already booked you on the early evening flight, but you will have to hurry,' Verity informed him with satisfaction.

'Have you?' he asked incredulously, looking up, his ice-blue eyes meeting hers with mutual respect and candour.

'Have a shower; if you give me your keys, I'll pick up your things,' instructed Verity as she pulled her long hair from her face and wrapped it in a ribbon, looking more the efficient secretary. If I'm going to take command, she thought, I'd better look the part. He gave her a half-smile of gratitude, and Verity's heart soared, though she masked her feelings behind her cool façade of professionalism.

'My passport is in my bedside locker,' he told her as she turned to leave.

'Right; I'll run you to the airport,' she called as she made her way to the door. She walked past the stunned Imogen, trying to hide her smile.

'Verity?' Saul waited till she turned to face him, then he said quietly, 'Come with me.' There was a plea in his voice, an anguish. Verity paused; she didn't know how to answer.

Imogen, who had remained silent, suddenly broke in, 'I'll come; it will be nice in France this time of year, and——'

'I haven't asked you, Imogen,' Saul stated coldly as he looked at her with disdain. He turned his attention back to Verity. 'Will you come? I need you.'

'I can't. Hannah...' she tried to explain.

'Please, Verity; I don't even know the language. If not for me, for Heloise...?'

'That's emotional blackmail.'

'Did it work?' he asked hopefully.

Verity didn't wait; she would have to think before answering him, and there was still so much to do. She left abruptly and felt a momentary pity for Imogen; she knew that Saul would never be able to forgive her for not relaying the message. He had virtually ignored her since the arrival of Verity, and he certainly had looked furious.

She looked at his car in horror—it was so sleek and large. Verity swallowed nervously and bit her bottom lip; would she be able to cope? She slid into the driver's seat and gave a sigh of relief; at least it was automatic. She smiled as she started the engine.

Verity had never seen Saul's home and, like everyone, she was impressed. It was a large detached residence with an imposing façade which was quite a contrast to the interior. The inside of the house, though very grand, had a warm, homely quality about it. It was furnished in very dark antique oak, solid and masculine like its owner, mused Verity as she hurried up the wide stairs, glancing through the large mullioned windows to see over the beautifully laid lawns.

The upstairs was as elaborate as down. There were numerous doors, and Verity peeped in every room. Each one was as beautifully decorated as the last—finally she found his room. She knew immediately it was his—the familiar smell of his aftershave hung in the air. It assailed Verity's nostrils and her stomach flipped as memories of him flooded back. The room was very large and had a huge window that gave a perfect view of the rolling countryside surrounding his house. There were numerous prints covering the walls—mostly of flowers or wildlife; was he that interested in the countryside? mused Verity as she looked at them. He had never given her that impression, but how much did she really know about him? Enough to know she was beginning to care for him.

Verity looked round and smiled. It was a well-kept room, smart, very elegant yet strong and dignified. As she opened the bedside cabinet her eyes alighted on a photograph of Heloise smiling out at her. Verity felt a stab of sorrow when she thought of the ailing child. Quickly she stopped her daydreaming and found his passport and stuffed it into her bag. She stretched up, reaching for his case from on top of the wardrobe. She then opened his drawers. Verity grabbed at socks, underwear, trousers and shirts, tossing them without much care into the case. There was a certain intimacy in packing the personal belongings of someone else, thought Verity as she tucked his toilet-bag down the sides and looked round frantically for a comb.

Finally, when she had collected together enough basics, she hurried back downstairs, flung the case into the boot, and drove back to town. She had one last thing to do before picking him up.

Saul was already waiting; he was striding up and down outside the mews, his long legs moving with an animal agility. He smiled the moment he saw her, but his face was pale, and dark shadows were apparent under his eyes, which lacked their usual sparkle. Verity felt her heart surge when she saw him; for once he looked vulnerable and lost, and she longed to comfort him.

'Why on earth didn't you wait inside? It would have been warmer,' she asked crossly as she leaned across and opened the car door.

'I can assure you the atmosphere in there is far from warm. In fact, it's decidedly frosty.' He laughed and sank back, closing his eyes. 'You seemed ages—what took you so long?'

'I went home to pick up a few things and to arrange with Mrs Collins about Hannah,' she explained, darting him a glance to see his reaction but trying to concentrate on the busy roads.

'You're coming, then? Oh, thank God!' His eyes shot open and he leaned towards her, pecking her gently on the cheek. 'Thanks, Verity—I'll make it up to you.'

'Dead right—I'm charging you double time!' she parried quickly, trying to disguise the electricity she felt every time he was near. Though it had been only a little kiss of friendship on her cheek, Verity's stomach had turned somersaults.

'Do you mind if I rest?' he asked apologetically, his eyes still shut.

'Not at all; I'm terrified driving this, it's so big and powerful, so I need to concentrate all I can,' she answered, her brow furrowed with anxiety as she manoeuvred the car around the hectic streets.

'You're doing fine; just relax and you'll enjoy it more,' he advised her.

Verity nodded in silence, but gripped the wheel all the same; it was years since she had driven and the roads were so much busier now. It was with much relief on her part that the car was finally parked and they began to walk to the airport.

'Have you eaten yet?' she asked Saul as the smell of fresh coffee reminded Verity she hadn't.

'No, I really don't think I could face it.'

'Because of the lobster or Heloise?'

'I don't know, I just feel...' He paused. 'How did you know about the lobster?'

'Imogen confessed,' she laughed. He reached out and gripped her hair, and Verity stiffened, her pulse vibrating. She felt the coolness of his hand on the nape of her neck and his touch was like a volt of electricity.

'Here, let's loosen that—I like to see your crowning glory.' He smiled as he shook her hair loose, tossing her dark locks in unruly waves across her shoulders.

'You have no idea how hard it is for Imogen to cook, although she tries,' he said, as if defending her.

'I find her very trying indeed,' retorted Verity, then more seriously she added, 'Will you be seeing her again?'

'I doubt it; we didn't part on good terms. Why?' he asked, his dark eyes looking at Verity with interest.

'I was curious to know if you would eat out in future.'
She tried to laugh but it caught in her throat.

'Certainly—if we see each other again I shall gladly
take her out to dinner.' He smiled, but Verity felt a stab
of regret that she had asked him. He picked up the cases
as Verity took their boarding-passes.

'I think you should have something. I know it's hard,
but it'll be better in the long run if you eat now,' she
told him gently, trying to dismiss any silly romantic
thoughts she was getting, and remembering she was here
in a professional capacity, nothing more.

'Why do you say that?' he asked, concerned.

'Look, Saul, we have no idea what's going on. Maybe
Heloise will be fine, but if not it's as well you have eaten,'
she added hurriedly.

'I see,' he said soberly.

'Come on; I'm sure she will be fine, and I'm starving.'
She clutched his arm as she spoke, feeling the taut
muscles rippling underneath his clothes, and propelled
him to the dining area.

'You know, you're quite bossy,' said Saul as he sipped
his coffee with amusement.

'Only when I have to be.'

'I think you're enjoying this.'

'A little.'

'Under different circumstances you would enjoy it a
lot,' he replied, nodding his head.

'Perhaps I would; maybe that's why I've never
married,' she laughed.

'No, that's not the reason,' he said, suddenly serious.
Verity coloured, and a *frisson* of excitement ran down
her spine.

'Then what is?'

'You are quite a——' he paused, as if searching for the right word '—independent—that's it—you're independent.'

'I have to be; there's no alternative.'

'But if there were, Verity? What then?' His eyes were alert with a compelling intensity.

'The situation has never arisen. I never get involved,' she replied, but a voice inside screamed, Until now!

'You hide underneath a façade of cool efficiency yet you are a very warm-hearted, tender person,' he finished as he emptied his cup, placing it down silently and watching Verity closely for her reaction.

'I have a little girl—I can hardly ignore that fact. Most men are not willing to take on another person's child.' She was feeling angry. Why did he question her like this? It had made it more than plain that he was not interested in her.

'You're almost like a child yourself——' he began, but Verity interrupted.

'I don't know what you mean. How can I possibly be like a child?' she asked indignantly but, when she thought of the sophisticated women he knew—like Imogen and Amanda—it was hardly surprising, she thought.

'Almost, I said almost. Don't get me wrong, Verity—I see you very much as a woman.'

If there was a compliment there Verity was unsure how to take it, so she gave a half-smile and lowered her head while she tried to sort out her jumbled thoughts.

They talked freely on the trip over. Verity commented on his prints and she was amazed to learn about his interest in the countryside, which even extended to his being a conservationist. They had telephoned Mr Ellis before leaving England, and by the time their plane had landed he was already there to meet them.

'What's happened?' snapped Saul anxiously once they were in the car and the usual pleasantries had been exchanged.

'We don't know; she had been complaining of tiredness, that's all,' he explained, the trauma apparent in his voice.

'Where is she now?'

'We telephoned Dr Claremont this morning, and he had her taken into the hospital immediately for tests. We're still awaiting those results,' he said sadly, and sighed wearily as he looked at the road ahead with blank eyes. He dropped them both off at the hospital then went back home to see his wife. 'We will be back later, Saul; phone if anything happens,' he said as he turned the car.

Saul was already marching into the hospital, so Verity called, 'Sure, as soon as we know anything.' She watched him drive away; he looked old. His wife had become ill with the shock of Heloise's admission to hospital and Verity thought perhaps they were becoming too old to care for a young child. She followed Saul into the hospital and swallowed as the usual hospital atmosphere assailed her nostrils. It was all so familiar to Verity—the tense, unspoken anxiety that they were both feeling, the sterile smell of disinfectant, the surge of hope and fear every time a door opened.

'Sit down, Saul; they'll let us know as soon as they know anything,' she commanded him, sitting him firmly down and passing him a paper cup of lukewarm coffee.

'It's the waiting; if I just knew something—anything,' he said, his harsh features growing even more hard with the anxiety.

'Don't fool yourself it's not anything you want to know. It's that everything is fine and everything will be fine,' reassured Verity, squeezing his hand and mentally praying that everything would be all right.

'Do you think so?' he asked, the cry for reassurance apparent on his drawn face.

'Yes, I do, but it's out of our hands at the moment.' Verity smiled as she spoke; she knew exactly how he was feeling, and the memories of how she had felt when it was Jonathan came rushing back. Yet she knew that since meeting Saul her feelings for Jonathan had changed; now he was just a pleasant memory.

'You think a lot of Heloise, don't you?' Verity asked.

'Yes, yes, I do; we were together for a long time before the divorce,' Saul said wistfully, his mind far-away, lost in some distant memories.

'I don't understand; why was she with you?' asked Verity, intrigued.

'You would like to know my lifestory?' he mocked, running his long fingers through his tousled mane of raven hair. Verity smiled and nodded.

'I'm quite sure it would be more interesting than his,' Verity said, disdainfully tossing a well-worn magazine article on the table. It carried the life story of a up-and-coming star.

'Possibly,' he remarked drily.

'So how come Heloise lived with you?' she asked— at least talking would occupy his mind, she thought.

'I have no family—well, none that cared. I left school and home the same day.' There was no regret in his voice—he could have been talking about someone else. Verity shuddered; it seemed odd to be so removed from one's own life.

'I started work for the Ellis company. It was a much smaller company then, and Marcus took a special interest in me. "The son I never had", he'd say. I met Amanda.' A wry smile broke out on Saul's face when he spoke her name, and Verity felt a stab of resentment. He sighed.

'She was having a steady relationship at the time with Étienne, but I don't think marriage was on his list, so I became flavour of the month. I was so besotted that I didn't realise I was being used. Amanda was just trying to make Étienne jealous. We married and went on honeymoon to France, where she met up with Étienne again.' He gave a hard laugh and Verity was instantly reminded of the antagonism between them.

'He wasted no time—Heloise was born the following year, and it was shortly after that I found Amanda and him in bed together.' Verity was stunned; it was a cruel betrayal, but at least her awareness of it now helped her understand Saul more.

'Amanda couldn't cope with a child—children are too demanding and she is too selfish. The château and vineyard seemed more attractive than me so she left; I refused to give her a divorce—injured pride, I suppose. I stayed with the Ellis company, determined to make it a success and myself as rich as the Bouvier family. Heloise stayed, and with her grandparents' help we managed without her mother.' The bitterness was still there in his voice and Verity felt sick that anyone could have left a child.

'So Heloise *is* your child?' asked Verity, instinctively knowing there was more. The grim expression on Saul's face confirmed it.

'No,' he said emphatically. 'You see, I had mumps at puberty; it was a severe attack and it left me...' He paused and swallowed. Verity reached out and took his hand, holding it gently, knowing how hard an admission like that would be.

'Amanda confirmed what I suspected; she told me Heloise was Étienne's, and she wanted her back—that I had no right to her. I gave her the divorce then—I had no option. There was a huge settlement on the condition that Heloise was to stay with her grandparents; Amanda agreed. Marcus retired to look after Heloise and I took over the company,' he finished.

'I came in at the Bouvier deal—yet another turn of the circle,' she concluded grimly.

There was little to say after that, but a thousand questions buzzed through Verity's mind. She couldn't believe that anyone would be so cruel, and yet if Amanda had lied in order to secure her divorce ... Verity tried to piece the story together in her own mind. She didn't want to get up any false hopes, and yet if there was a chance, no matter how remote, surely she must tell him ...

Verity cast a glance at Saul. He looked tired, his face was pale and drawn, but she was looking more closely, looking for clues—any shadow of a resemblance. The silence was electrifying and the doctor, after he had spoken to them, realising that they needed time, left them alone to think about what he had just told them.

Heloise was suffering from a severe form of anaemia; though she had been given iron intra-muscularly, she was very weak and really needed a transfusion. Unfortunately she was also of a very rare blood-group. The possibility of finding a match was remote; in previous cases, parents had already been checked at their local hospitals.

Verity knew then she had no choice; no matter how slim the chance, it might save Heloise's life. Saul was growing more agitated; he was striding around the waiting-room, his footsteps echoing around them. Verity knew he had to take that blood test. 'There must be someone?' yelled Saul. 'For God's sake, this type of information should be on computer,' he raged, his eyes soft with unshed tears.

'Calm down, Saul; they're doing all they can,' interjected Verity.

'Yes, I know,' he said wearily, sinking into a chair, his face deathly white, his lips taut and pale.

'Saul, have your blood checked,' Verity suddenly said, her eyes bright.

'Me? Why? Don't be silly.'

'You must, you must now! Please, Saul.'

'Look Verity, there's no point. They might as well check your group.'

'Right, OK. Let's do it. I'll have mine checked too,' she insisted.

'Why, Verity? It's——'

'It's Heloise's life; you must do it!' Verity was determined, her eyes fixed on Saul's, almost daring him to argue.

'You're bossy.'

'Just do it now; please, Saul.'

Verity paced silently up and down, wringing her hands in anxiety. She hoped she was right; she felt sure she was. She bit into her bottom lip and thought hard. It had to be true—there was no other explanation. After what she felt was an eternity, the door suddenly swept open and there stood Saul. There was no need for words, Saul rushed towards Verity, now understanding why she'd been so insistent. They fell into each other's arms, clinging to each other as if they were drowning.

'She's mine, she's always been mine!' Saul cried as he hugged Verity so tightly that he hurt.

'I know, I know,' whispered Verity softly in his ear and gently stroking his hair. She could smell the aromatic scent of his masculine aftershave, and was cruelly aware of the closeness of their two bodies.

'I'm so pleased for you,' Verity said, trying to release herself for fear her body would betray the effect he was having on her.

'Oh, Verity, how can I ever thank you?' he cried, clasping her face in his hands and lifting it till he could see her. Verity trembled, her eyes dilating as she met his vivid ice-blue eyes. She swallowed hard as her heart-rate increased.

'What's happening to Heloise?' she asked sharply, trying to regain her composure, and she felt him stiffen at her tone.

'What's wrong, Verity?' he replied gently, his hands still holding her face.

'Nothing,' she answered, too quickly. 'I just want to know.'

He released her immediately and stepped back, and Verity felt a cold chill as their bodies lost contact.

'They want to take some of my blood——' he shrugged his powerful shoulders lazily '—no problem!'

'When?'

'They'll call for me any minute. Will you wait?'

'Of course.'

'I'll arrange for a private room; you go and buy some food. I'll need it afterwards,' he said, the radiance of his smile piercing her heart.

* * *

The private room the nurse showed Verity to was quite dark. The last few rays of sunlight filtered through, marking the bed in black stripes. Verity closed the door silently and placed the shopping on the floor. She crept over to the bedside; her heart was beating so fast that she felt sure it was audible. Saul was sleeping; and his slow, relaxed breathing soothed Verity's nerves. She leaned over the bed; his dark hair had fallen into his eyes and very gently Verity pushed it away. She smiled at the sleeping form. He looked pale, his eyes a little sunken. The tiredness was etched on his face, yet it could not mask his handsome features. She sat down on a chair beside his bed and tried to read the paperback novel she had brought, but her eyes constantly strayed to his face. He was always asleep, and Verity too felt herself drifting off as the evening drew in. She must have dozed off because when she awoke the blinds were firmly closed and a bedside lamp was on.

'Oh!' gasped Verity in surprise when she looked up to see Saul staring at her. He gave her a slow smile that transformed his face. He looked alive and bright, almost his usual self.

'Did I surprise you? I'm sorry, I've been watching you for some time,' he said, propping himself upright as he spoke.

'Have you?' asked Verity, beginning to colour, and grateful for the semi-darkness, as it would not be visible.

'Hmm,' he said thoughtfully, resting back on his pillows and closing his eyes again.

'Are you allowed to eat and drink?' Verity asked cautiously as she jerked her head in the direction of the shopping-bags.

'Doctor's orders!' he laughed, sitting upright again and leaning out of the bed in order to see what she had brought.

'It's not much—the local shops aren't that good.'

'Not that good?' laughed Saul in disbelief. 'Where on earth would you find food like this in your average local English shop?'

'You're right,' agreed Verity as she emptied the bag. She had bought a chicken terrine, fresh salad, a crusty French loaf, with a Brie that was so ripe that it had oozed out of its wrapper and, to finish, a beautiful *tarte aux pommes* and a large bottle of the local grape juice.

'It's a feast!' roared Saul, breaking off a large chunk of bread; then his face fell. 'No knives, no bottle opener.'

'Oh, ye of little faith,' admonished Verity, shaking her head. 'The bottle has a screw-top and I bought a plastic picnic set from the local garage.'

'You certainly think of everything, don't you?' he spoke softly, a tenderness in his voice she had longed to hear but didn't expect. Verity's alarm system started to ring. Steady, girl—he is under stress.

'That's what you pay me for,' she retorted briskly.

'No, not today—you've really helped me today. I don't know what I would have done without you,' he said earnestly, moving slightly towards her as he spoke.

'I know what it's like; you feel as if someone has just clubbed you over the head, and yet every nerve in your body is screaming,' she explained, shifting so that she could move further away without him noticing.

'Yes,' he replied thoughtfully, 'I'd forgotten you've been through this. Are those memories still as painful?'

'No, not at all, and Hannah more than makes up,' replied Verity, suddenly longing to be at home, safe, where her life was neat and in a pattern. Yet since knowing Saul nothing had been the same.

'This juice is good; have some more,' said Saul, tipping the bottle into Verity's glass.

'Thanks!' she laughed as she jumped from her chair to mop up the spillage.

'Sorry; here, let me kiss you better,' he mocked, pulling her across the bed towards him with remarkable ease. Verity fell clumsily next to him and immediately tried to get up. They were far too close for comfort and she could feel her heart racing. He drew her trembling hand upwards towards his mouth and began to kiss and lick the wet red juice from the back of her hand. Verity smiled weakly down at him, her whole body alive, tingling with anticipation. He drew her down upon himself and their bodies fused together. Somehow his arms crept up around her, drawing her closer, and she felt herself being drawn towards him as if by an unseen magnet. He raised his arms seductively, stroking her back. His warm breath brushed the side of her face; she could feel it against her cheek. Then his lips caressed the corner of her mouth— the touch was gentle and faintly teasing. The tip of his tongue edged the soft outline of her lips with a feather-light touch that made her ache for more. Her whole body became alive, vibrant, moving towards him in silent admission of defeat. She could fight him no longer; she had neither the strength or inclination. She parted her lips, unconsciously inviting his possession of her that she was offering so willingly. She sought his mouth; at first it was soft, persuasive, then it hardened, becoming more demanding.

They drew closer together, the need for each other overwhelming. The kiss was hungry yet incredibly gentle.

Verity was slowly losing all sense of reality; all that mattered was the here and now. The grim reality that surrounded them seemed fantasy. They needed each other so much; he let his mouth descend to her throat and she arched her head back in response. His tongue traced a path to her throat and she moaned softly as she felt the coolness of the room chill her breasts. He had unbuttoned her blouse with expert ease and slipped his hand under her strap, pulling her bra gently away from her. He cupped her breast, stroking it with a firmness that was gentle but masterful. Verity's body melted into a sea of desire as Saul began a teasing exploration of her rosy-peaked breasts. A slow ache was awoken in her that needed fulfilment—yet it was not right.

He didn't love her, he only wanted her, and after the trauma of the day it was often a very natural response in many people. To want to hold on to someone to feel that closeness was reassuring. No, no, Verity cried inwardly as her body continued to respond to his delicate probings. His strong arm wrapped around her slim waist, pulling her so close that she could feel his hardness against her. Verity gave a slight gasp of surprise but his mouth joined hers immediately to stifle any protests. Her whole body began to vibrate as it instinctively reacted to the firm action of his hands as they caressed her naked skin. Verity buried her face in his chest, breathing in deeply his musky scent, completely unaware that the door had opened and a shadowy figure was watching them. The light illuminated the room with a sharp brilliance. Verity stiffened and turned in horror to see Amanda Bouvier watching them both with a cold, flint-eyed look.

CHAPTER NINE

'PERHAPS my apology was a little premature,' Amanda said frostily, viewing Verity with contempt. The icy tone in her voice was matched with the glacial look she was giving them both. The sudden brightness of the light troubled Verity's eyes and she sat up immediately and began to draw her blouse around her, fastening her buttons with clumsy fingers. Amanda watched her with mild interest, which flustered Verity all the more. Whatever must she think of me—first her husband, now Saul? Verity coloured as she thought of the only conclusion she would come to if she were in Amanda's position.

The silence was pregnant and Verity longed for Saul to say something. She raised her eyes to look at him, but he had lain back in his bed, the back of his head resting on his hands, his eyes closed. He did not appear in the least bit interested in Verity's dilemma. She felt herself colour, though she wasn't sure whether it was due to embarrassment or anger. Did Saul care for her or had he just been using her—was he now embarrassed by what had just happened? She willed him to speak, to say to her how much he loved her; but he remained silent.

'I had no idea your secretary had so many talents; it must be so handy for those long business trips,' Amanda mocked, her eyes narrowing to diamond chips and her mouth becoming a thin, cruel line. Verity stiffened at

the implication of the remark, and felt sure that Saul
would jump to her defence.

'What do you want, Amanda?' barked Saul, not
bothering to open his eyes.

'Well, I can see you're busy, but I thought Heloise
was more of a priority.'

'You hypocrite!' growled Saul. 'Heloise has never been
a priority to you.'

'It was you, Saul, who insisted on separating us. I
wanted Heloise,' she said coolly, the atmosphere becoming tense. She shrugged her slim shoulders and inclined her head to the door. 'I think you had better leave,'
she instructed Verity, who was only too glad to get away.

'No, stay Verity; we have nothing to discuss,' snapped
Saul, his eyes opening for the first time to look at her;
but his expression was unfathomable.

'I think you have, Saul; if you both care so much for
Heloise, I suggest you will have to talk and sort something out,' Verity explained, thinking only of the poor
little girl who was being squabbled over as if she were
a toy. Saul sat up and leaned over towards Verity; she
could feel his warm breath on her face.

'Do you really think that would be for the best?' he
asked sincerely. Verity nodded, but did not want to stay;
she wanted to run to put as much distance as she could
between her and Saul. She was too aware of his masculinity; even now his very nakedness aroused her.
Amanda sauntered over to the bed, her eyes fixed on
Saul, her face gentle and tender.

'Saul, I know what you have been through, but let's
try to forget the past for now,' she said, taking his hand
in a gesture of friendship.

'The past has certainly come back to haunt us, Amanda,' he jeered as he looked at her intently.

'We must talk; I didn't know—I thought...' She paused and flashed a look at Verity. 'This really is private,' she said, almost pleading.

'I think I'll go; I've booked a room at the local hotel,' flustered Verity as she ran from the room. She felt a million hot pin-heads prick at the back of her eyes as she ran from the hospital.

The next morning Verity returned to the hospital with a feeling of anticipation. Surely now that everything was settled Saul would be ready to make a commitment to her? She smiled as she recalled last night, the two of them entwined, totally in love. She made her way to Saul's room with light, easy steps. She was longing to see him. She opened the door cautiously. It was empty except for a breakfast tray, which had been set for two people. Verity frowned, then noticed how the room was filled with the heavy sexy perfume of Amanda. It was obvious they had spent the night here together. She darted a look at the bed; had they? she wondered, suddenly frightened.

'Verity?' a familiar voice sounded behind her, and she turned to face Saul. He looked well—very well. The colour had returned to his face, his eyes held a brightness that she hadn't seen before. She smiled, and was about to rush into his arms, when he said, 'We had a long talk last night, and I think we have reached a decision. Amanda has apologised about barging in—well, of course, she didn't expect——'

Verity interrupted immediately, masking her feelings at once. 'I hope you're not going to apologise for last night; there's no need. It was natural in the circumstances,' she said quickly, not noticing how his face had darkened as she spoke.

'In the circumstances?' he repeated, his eyes flashing.

'You were under a lot of stress; it happens.' She shrugged her shoulders in an attempt to appear casual.

'And you're an expert in such matters,' he taunted, the grim expression on his face becoming even grimmer. Verity flushed, puzzled by his annoyance.

'I remember when Jonathan died I felt the need to hold someone; I had my family for support——'

'And I only had you,' he interjected. 'How convenient.'

'Let's not go into it; it really isn't that important,' Verity answered, amazed by the composure in her voice when her insides were in a turmoil and her heart cried out for him to say something.

'"Isn't that important"? What do you mean?'

'Just that, Saul; these things happen, remember—like in France when I was distressed. It doesn't mean anything,' lied Verity, her heart breaking in two when he accepted what she said so easily.

'I see,' he said coldly, viewing her with a furrowed brow. 'I don't think Amanda saw it quite like that, though.'

'Perhaps it would be better if I left now, then... Where's Amanda?' asked Verity, not wishing to face her.

'With Heloise; they get on quite well, which is amazing,' he said in disbelief.

'Does Heloise understand you're her real father now?' asked Verity, not wanting to hear about Amanda, and trying to remind him of the deceit.

Saul shrugged. 'We have decided not to say anything yet—there's so much to sort out.'

'Hmm, I suppppose there must,' mused Verity resentfully.

'Come on; Heloise wants to see you.'

'Oh—I'm not sure, Saul,' Verity faltered.

'Please; I'd like you two to like each other,' he begged. Verity nodded silently, then she smiled and followed him down the corridor, her heart aching with every step she took. She watched his every move and the memories of his body next to hers tormented her. They had been so passionate, so abandoned, and yet to him it was nothing. She loved him, she knew that, but she derived no consolation in knowing it, as it was not returned.

'Do you know who this is?' burst out Heloise the second Verity went through the door. Heloise's face was still drawn and pale but the pleasure made her eyes glow. 'Do you?' she asked again, longing to make the introductions.

Verity stole a glance at Amanda, and her heart melted. She had wanted to hate her, to see her as a selfish, spoilt woman who cared for no one—but she couldn't. There was no glamour to her bare face; her eyes were leaden with the worry of her child, and at that moment Verity felt a rapport between them. Though they were not at all alike yet they were still both mothers, and that bond seemed to be more important than anything at that moment. Verity smiled.

'Who is she?' asked Verity, not wishing to spoil Heloise's fun.

'This is my mother. She is a very important fashion writer; that's why I don't see her often,' the little girl explained. Verity extended her hand in a gesture of friendship, not knowing how the other woman would react. They shook hands, but there was no real warmth in the action.

'You'll see a lot more of me now, though, since Saul and I have sorted things out,' Amanda said, leaning across the bed towards Saul. 'Haven't we?'

Verity felt a stab of pain just at that one word—'we.' Saul and Amanda, the parents of this child. She smiled, directing it at Heloise. 'That's wonderful,' she said with a tremble in her voice.

'Yes, isn't it?' agreed Amanda, flashing a set of perfectly white teeth at Saul.

'Is it?' questioned Saul abruptly as he drew Heloise into his arms, hugging her closely. Verity's heart sank even further; the isolation she felt made her feel cold and she longed to be back with Hannah, to feel her little warm reassuring arms around her. She cast a swift glance at Saul, but his head was bent downwards as he kissed the cheeks of Heloise while she rested in his arms. Verity felt a stab of jealousy, but she smiled warmly when he raised his head and met her gaze. Heloise listened attentively to the tales her mother told and Verity, despite herself, could not help but laugh at the amusing anecdotes. Saul sat silently, almost sullen, but he smiled indulgently at Heloise, stroking her hand affectionately till Verity could stand it no longer.

'I'll have to be getting back, Saul, if that's all right?' she asked, determined to go whether he liked it or not.

'Yes, why not? Thanks for all your help, but I understand your wanting to get home.' His face was set starkly, his mouth tight and compressed; he showed her none of the gentleness he had lavished on Amanda and Heloise.

Understand? You don't know the meaning of the word! she wanted to scream at him, but instead she smiled faintly and said with her usual efficiency, 'Right, well, I'll book a flight for today.'

'Could you possibly stay with Heloise for a while? We want to go and see my parents. Circumstances have now changed, you see,' purred Amanda.

Verity felt herself colour, and she had to force her eyes not to fill. 'Of course; I'll be glad to stay,' replied Verity as she watched them start to leave, Amanda slipping her arm through Saul's in a gesture of union. The pain was almost unbearable; Saul flashed her a smile, but instead of the usual joy it only brought pain. She looked at him, suddenly so aware of how much he meant to her, and she tried to return the smile, but she couldn't. Instead she nodded numbly.

Heloise turned excitedly towards Verity. 'I shall be coming to England now—maybe even going to school there. Mummy is hoping to get a transfer to London.'

'Is she? That will be good,' replied Verity, her heart sinking at the words. What had happened to Étienne? she wondered.

'There's so much going on in the London fashion scene,' said Heloise, obviously repeating what her mother had told her.

'Rest now; you're still very tired,' said Verity softly as she settled the little girl to sleep. She did not want to hear any more. It hurt her too much. Heloise soon fell asleep and Verity sat beside her bed idly flicking through a pile of magazines; but her mind was filled with thoughts of Saul.

'I'm back,' whispered Saul as he entered the room.

Verity jumped in surprise. 'Is everything OK?' she asked, vitally aware of his body, the musky scent of his aftershave.

'Well, there's still a lot to sort out, but we are getting there,' he replied, sitting down on the bed, his legs accidentally touching Verity's. The stimulus it gave her was like a jolt of electricity, and she moved her legs quickly away. She tucked them under her chair and Saul frowned at her action.

'I think it's for the best; most children are better with two parents, aren't they?' he asked, his dark eyes fixed on Verity's, awaiting her response.

'I'm hardly the right person to ask,' she snapped back bitterly.

'Yes, of course you are—you do want to get married, don't you?' He sounded puzzled and a frown creased his forehead as he looked intently at Verity.

'I haven't really thought about it, but I wouldn't marry just to give Hannah a father. That would be too risky,' she explained, amazed at the calmness of her voice when her mind was crying out to him, I love you, I'd marry you!

'What do you mean, "risky"?' he snapped, his eyes growing darker and more forbidding.

'There's no need to start getting angry. Marriage is a commitment based on the love of two people. Children normally come later, by mutual agreement.'

'I see,' he said tightly. 'You mean if the child already exists it wouldn't work?'

'It could, but I don't know whether I'd be prepared to take that step,' she said, unaware of the impact her words were making.

'Does that mean you will never marry?'

'No, I may do one day, but not for a long time yet,' she answered, but in her mind she added, Because it will take me so long to get over you.

'You still feel a great deal for Jonathan?' Saul said as he rose from the bed.

'I am in love, very much in love—I can't help it,' she answered honestly. It was better he thought it was Jonathan—it saved any embarrassment.

'When are you leaving?'

'This afternoon,' she answered him, trying to make her voice sound bright.

'Then you will join Amanda and me for lunch?' he stated, his voice cold. It was more an order than a request.

'I don't think so; I've my packing to do and——'

'Don't be ridiculous! Go and pack now, and we'll pick you up at your hotel and take you straight to the airport for your flight after lunch.'

'Right, I'll go now,' said Verity, longing to be away from him—especially now, when it was more than plain that he and Amanda seemed to be getting on so well.

The drive to the restaurant was through the beautiful green countryside, but it flashed before Verity's eyes; not a blade of grass warranted her attention. The scene seemed to pass before her eyes in a relentless, boring image. She felt too numb to do or think of anything. It was a hopeless situation, she thought to herself, shaking her head. She couldn't believe she had acted so foolishly, and Saul was more than willing to dismiss the whole incident. Verity almost felt grateful that Amanda had interrupted them.

The journey seemed long—endless. Amanda seemed to talk incessantly and Saul was cool and distant. 'You're very quiet, Verity,' he commented for the hundredth time, but Verity only gave a half-smile in reply. Saul frowned at the rebuff and concentrated on the road ahead. Verity's mind was in a turmoil. What was there to say, what did he want—her congratulations, perhaps? she thought bitterly.

At last they reached the restaurant; it was a beautiful place perched high up in the hills. It seemed to be clinging to the side of the hill tempting providence by not falling into the vast ravine. They sat outside enjoying the fresh air and sipping an aperitif. Verity viewed the menu uninterestedly. She chose a simple grilled fish with fennel and fresh vegetables. The food was probably perfect, but what little Verity ate tasted like cardboard. Saul ate well, as usual—nothing had upset his appetite, thought Verity bitterly as she toyed with her fish. Verity sensed that Saul was watching her despite the fact that Amanda kept up a non-stop conversation the whole time. She raised her eyes but kept her head lowered and she stole a quick glance at him.

His face, though sharp-featured, was softened by the warmth in his dark eyes, and his mouth was relaxed into a slow, sensuous curve that made her heart flutter. She sipped at her white wine, trying hard to think about the conversation going on around her, but it was impossible. She was too numb. She gazed out of the window, her eyes fixed on the distant horizon in a bid to remain calm.

'Are you sure you're all right?' asked Saul. 'I bet it's a migraine starting; I'll go and get you something.' Verity's protest fell on deaf ears, and Saul strode away.

She smiled weakly at Amanda, who stared back at her, her eyes troubled.

'You really have worked wonders on him, haven't you?' she said.

'Have I?' asked Verity with a frown.

'Oh, yes, I can't begin to explain.' Then she shrugged her shoulders and gave a laugh. 'We were so much younger then—too much passion, not enough sense.' Verity didn't reply; there didn't seem to be anything suitable to say. Amanda continued, 'He is very fond of Heloise, and she adores him. Most women adore him— he is terribly attractive.'

'Yes, I suppose so,' Verity answered, wishing she were a million miles away.

'I am ever so grateful to you; it was your intervention that saved my daughter's life. Saul was livid but I hadn't deliberately deceived him at the time—well, it's all so long ago,' she said dismissively. Verity nodded in reply and stared at Amanda; she was far prettier than she had previously realised, and her easygoing manner made it difficult for Verity to dislike her as much as she wanted to.

'I think, under the circumstances, I shall be returning to London; at least I should have a permanent base there now,' she continued. Verity stiffened, her heart beating rapidly; what Heloise had said about her mother coming to England seemed to be true, not just wishful thinking on the little girl's part.

'You're really thinking of coming to England?' she asked, her heart sinking even further.

'Oh, yes, didn't Saul explain? Étienne and I are separated now, and I have decided to find a home in London for Heloise's sake.' She laughed again. 'It's taken me a long time to realise what I was missing, but better late than never.'

'Yes, that's true; I'm sure you will be very happy together,' mumbled Verity, nearly choking on the words.

'Who will be happy?' interrupted Saul as he sauntered back over, with his usual relaxed ease.

'I will when I find somewhere suitable to live in England,' answered Amanda, gazing up at Saul adoringly.

'No doubt you will,' he agreed frostily, then he turned to look at Verity and passed her a packet of tablets. 'Here you are,' he said; their hands touched momentarily and a jolt of electricity soared through Verity. She looked up swiftly and met his look head-on. She felt herself colouring but she was trapped by the intensity of his gaze, and she was forced to look at him. Her mouth went dry as she looked at him, and her heart skipped a beat as familiar feelings stirred within her.

'Thank you,' she managed to mutter as she took the tablets from his hand. Verity was grateful when the meal ended and they sat drinking coffee. It had been difficult to sit next to Saul knowing that she had lost him to Amanda, but perhaps it was for the best, she tried to convince herself, at least for little Heloise.

As if reading her thoughts, Amanda said suddenly, 'You do like Heloise, don't you?'

'Yes, of course,' smiled Verity. 'I have a little girl myself of a similar age.'

'That's right; Saul did mention that to me, and they have met each other, haven't they?' she asked curiously.

'For a little while. They seemed to get on very well,' agreed Verity, wondering where the conversation was leading.

'Good,' nodded Amanda, and said nothing else.

Verity shot a glance at Saul for some explanation, but he just flashed her a smile. Verity felt a stab of annoyance; she had always considered Saul a difficult man, yet he was behaving *so* insensitively—she found it unbelievable. The delicate desserts arrived—a fluffy sweet omelette filled with luscious ripe strawberries and covered in cognac-flavoured cream. Normally Verity would have enjoyed such a dish, but she shook her head miserably when Saul offered her one. He looked slightly hurt for a moment, but Amanda soon demanded his undivided attention again.

Verity watched them both with a morbid curiosity. They suited each other, she had to confess—both worldly socialites, each attractive in their own way. She glanced down at her simple clothing—shirt and trousers—compared to the immaculate tailored suit Amanda was wearing. She felt almost ashamed, and she took up her wine glass, unaware of how much she had been drinking, yet Saul gave her a frown of disapproval. The wine was numbing the pain she felt; it raced through her body, giving warmth and life where she felt nothing.

'Do you like France?' asked Amanda, trying to draw Verity into conversation. Verity was unsettled for a moment; France held too many memories for her now. She took another mouthful of wine before answering.

'I travelled in France a great deal when I was a student, with Jonathan.' Amanda looked puzzled for a moment.

'Oh, I forgot you don't know about Jonathan; he was Hannah's father—he's dead,' Verity stated, drinking more wine and becoming more reckless. 'We always took our holidays in France till Jonathan decided it was all too unadventurous.' Verity gave a hollow laugh when

she remembered how Jonathan had changed. 'He decided, or rather a friend of his decided, they should go
mountain climbing. Poor Jonathan—he wanted to fit in
so badly.' Verity paused, lost in her own memories; ab-
sently she leaned across the table to take up the bottle
of wine again, but Saul moved it before her hand touched
it. Verity's head shot up with temper.

'Please refill my glass,' she said, offering it to Saul.
He stared back at her grimly, his dark eyes warning her
to be silent, but the wine had instilled too much confidence in her. 'I want more wine,' she demanded, a slight
slur to her voice.

'You've had more than enough,' Saul retorted, his
voice low and threatening. Their eyes met, locked in
conflict.

If anger is the only emotion I can raise in him, then
damn it, I will! thought Verity as she spoke louder. 'I
should like more wine—now!' she ordered Saul, and his
eyes swept swiftly around the other diners. Then he reluctantly passed her the bottle.

'Thank you,' goaded Verity, a smile of triumph on
her face, although inwardly she felt desolate.

Amanda stood looking slightly embarrassed by the
proceedings. 'I shall go to freshen up,' she smiled.

'Isn't that a bit risky, leaving me here alone with him?'
Verity inclined her head over towards Saul as she spoke.
'I mean, first there was Étienne, then last night——'
Verity got no further; Saul moved with lightning speed
and before his movements had even registered with Verity
he had grabbed her by the arm.

'Shut up!' he hissed; his dark eyes looked forbidding
and the austere expression on his face pierced through

Verity's alcoholic haze to make her realise she had gone too far.

'I'll take her to the car,' Saul called to Amanda as he virtually dragged Verity outside. The cool fresh air hit Verity with such an impact that she felt sick; she was spinning around and around and she was grateful that a pair of strong arms seemed to be supporting her. Saul propelled her over to a grassy bank, where she sank down in a graceless heap. The whole place seemed to be spinning at an enormous rate and Verity felt as if she too was being lifted up and spun. She groaned and held her sticky, hot head.

'You damned fool!' Saul's voice grated beside her. 'What on earth did you go and do that for?' he growled as he squatted down beside her. Verity shook her head but stopped immediately as it only added to her discomfort. She had no idea how long she was forced to sit there, but the spinning seemed never to stop. She could hear Amanda and Saul talking, but whatever they were saying was no longer registering with her.

'I feel a little better now,' she said quietly like an apologetic child, and they both turned to look at her pale face. Saul gave a wry smile but he was still angry— Verity could tell by the hard line of his jaw. He put her into the back of the car with both windows rolled down completely by way of a precaution. Verity mumbled an apology to Amanda, but the woman was gracious enough just to acknowledge it with a smile and a slight nod of the head.

'I hope to see you again,' Amanda called to Verity as the car drove away and, though Verity smiled back, she thought, I hope I never see you again!

'How are you feeling now?' asked Saul, peering at her through his car mirror.

'OK, I guess; I don't know...' She stopped. She knew full well why she had drunk too much—to say otherwise would be a lie.

'What do you think of Amanda?' asked Saul, his eyes fixed on the road ahead.

'I don't know her well enough to pass an opinion,' Verity answered, amazed at her composure.

'I think she genuinely cares for Heloise, which is surprising, don't you think?' Verity didn't answer; it was none of her business and she felt if she said anything her own feelings might be revealed.

'I'm glad she has decided to offer Heloise some stability. Perhaps you could ring round a few estate agents, try and find a couple of suitable properties to view?' he continued, unaware of the pain he was causing. Verity shuddered; it was as if she had been stabbed and now, with slow deliberation, he was turning the knife.

'What about your house?' she snapped. He roared with laughter, throwing his head back.

'Amanda in that house—in the country? No way!'

'She prefers the city life?'

'Yes, I guess so—and you, Verity, what do you prefer?' he asked, suddenly serious, looking at her with a direct, unwavering gaze.

'I should love to live away from the city, to bring Hannah up among the fresh air, to have enough money to stop working and just enjoy being a mother,' she answered truthfully.

'I thought you were a career girl,' he drawled.

'I have to work to support myself and Hannah—you know that. I haven't any choice,' she retorted briskly.

'But if given a choice you're not willing to take the risk?' he asked coldly as they drew up outside the airport.

'I'm not willing to marry just for Hannah's sake. I would have to love the man I married,' she replied as she took the case from his hand, totally aware of him and yet hiding all her feelings to the point of becoming brusque.

'Are you capable of loving any man, Verity?' Saul asked, then, without pausing, he continued, 'Because I'm not sure you will be ever ready for that commitment.'

'And you are?'

'Yes,' he stated emphatically, looking at her intently, his dark eyes boring into her. Verity lowered her gaze and turned away.

'Shall I come to the checking-in desk with you?' he asked, but Verity knew he longed to be back with Amanda and Heloise.

'No, that's all right—I'll manage,' she replied stiffly.

'I'll see you some time next week; rearrange what meetings you can or cancel them,' he said as she turned to go, red-hot pin-heads pricking the back of her eyes. 'Verity?' He spoke her name so softly that she turned despite herself.

She looked at him, longing to be in his arms, yet she said coolly, 'Is there something else, Mr Easton?'

His eyes darkened for a moment, then he shrugged his powerful shoulders, called, 'Take care!', then climbed back in his car and drove away.

Verity watched him drive off in silence, then the tears began to flow—hot tears splashing down her face, her body shaking uncontrollably as the strength of her hidden emotions spilled out at last.

CHAPTER TEN

THE sky was grey and leaden, and, as Verity's eyes swept miserably over her damp flat, she felt sure she had made the right decision. She had never imagined herself leaving England—she enjoyed its green fields too much to sacrifice them for the sun. Yet Australia seemed more attractive with each passing day.

It had been over a week since she had seen Saul, but his absence seemed only to increase her feeling of sorrow. Yet Verity was unsure how she would react once they were together again. She bit her bottom lip, her eyes filling with unshed tears, making them look sore and bloodshot. She had cried so many tears that she was amazed that she still had any to shed...

She rushed through the office door, dripping wet; the rain had poured relentlessly since her return to England, and it matched her mood completely. She shivered with the cold; the office was quiet, deadly quiet, and Verity gave a sigh of relief; he was not in again. Would he return this week? she pondered as she crossed the office.

She felt a stab of sorrow as she thought about the rest of her life stretching out endlessly before her. It all seemed so empty now, and she felt terribly alone and dejected. She had tried to be positive, but it was hopeless; she had fallen head over heels despite herself. The moment she had met him she had been instinctively on her guard—she'd known this man threatened her equilibrium. He was so unlike any other man she had met before, and once she'd begun to compare him to Jonathan she'd realised that her love for Jonathan—though sweet—had been young. Jonathan had never thrilled her the way Saul could, by the merest touch or his radiating smile.

These thoughts had raced a million times through her head till she could only think of one solution—to put as much distance as possible between her and Saul. She had decided to make a complete break—to emigrate to Australia to be with her parents and brother; she desperately needed them now. Verity knew she could not possibly go on working with Saul, yet the thought of never seeing him again filled her with equal anguish. She knew she looked pale; she hadn't been sleeping well since her return to England, and she seemed to have no appetite at all.

She cast a cursory glance in the mirror at her dull reflection. The brightness of her sapphire eyes was certainly dimmed, and, though she had taken the trouble to apply blusher to give her cheeks some colour, it merely seemed to emphasise the paleness of the rest of her complexion. She stared mutely at her reflection, the generous curve of her mouth seeming slightly at odds with the sorrow she felt inside.

She hung her coat up, shaking the rain from it as she did so. She had lost her umbrella, her mind being constantly preoccupied with other thoughts. The beautiful mantle of thick hair, normally carefully secured high up on her head, fell limply around her shoulders, and hung in a wet sheet against her face. Verity pushed it away, yet it drooped down in a wet mass and she did not have the incentive to do anything more to it. She sat down wearily at her desk and sighed; she had never been so unhappy in all her life. She began to file through the mail and sort it into several different piles; there was nothing urgent. The pace of the office had virtually come to a standstill in Saul's absence.

Then she started. Surely it couldn't be him? He would have telephoned to let her know of his return. Verity felt a growing sense of panic as she heard the lift doors glide open. She knew instinctively that it was him, and began to tremble. Her mouth went dry, her mind a blank. She tried to concentrate on the contents of the letter in front of her, but the words seemed to run together as she heard his approach.

'Good morning, Verity,' he said briskly as he entered the office. Verity stiffened; she hadn't expected him back yet, and the warm sound of his voice made her acutely aware of how she felt. The very sound of his voice was an inexplicable source of joy. She looked up quickly to see the amused lights dance in his dark eyes. He looked as handsome as ever, she thought. He was wearing a beautifully tailored navy suit offset by a snowy-white shirt. The immaculate way he was presented only emphasised Verity's poor appearance. She suddenly wished she looked better, but it was too late now, and he wasn't interested in her anyway.

'I didn't expect you back so soon,' she admitted nervously, trying to clear her thoughts as they all jostled together in her mind. She had hoped she would be more in control next time they met, but his very closeness seemed to rob her of any sense.

'You don't look well,' he said, and his dark eyes appeared troubled as they made a slow, critical appraisal of her. 'Have you lost weight?' he asked, a furrow creasing his brow. For some reason his concern angered her; was it sincere, or merely a polite enquiry he would have made to any old employee?

'Yes, I have, but quite deliberately—I needed to lose some weight,' she lied. Yet her heart cried out, I can no longer sleep or eat because of you—you dominate my every waking moment and intrude into my snatches of sleep!

'Rubbish!' he barked. 'You had no need to lose any weight.'

Verity wondered whether that was a compliment or merely an observation. She raised her eyes to look at him and her heart leapt; his dark suit could not hide the muscular strength of the man. How she hated the way her own body constantly responded to him! It was a betrayal, yet she had no control.

'What's the matter?' he questioned again, his dark eyes watching her with perceptive scrutiny.

'Not a thing; maybe the weather is just getting me down!' She tried to laugh but it caught in her throat. 'If you go through I'll get all the papers to bring you up to date.'

She was grateful when he disappeared into his office as it gave her a few minutes to relax, so that when she finally entered she could present a cool façade that belied the turmoil she felt inside. When she went in he was sitting lounging in his chair, his hands folded at the back of his head and his long legs stretched out before him, crossed casually at the ankle. The weak autumn sun cast a shadow on his face, making him look even more attractive, mused Verity. She faltered at the door for a moment, aware that he was watching her every move.

'You seem a little nervous,' he drawled as he took the sheaf of papers from her shaking hand. His eyes travelled upwards to meet her face, and Verity knew she had blushed despite herself. She had to keep her cool; she could not afford to allow her feelings to become known.

'There are several properties here that I think might be suitable for Amanda,' she replied, trying to ignore the goading tone in his voice. She hated herself for looking for homes for them, but did not want him to know. Yet the hostility was present in her eyes.

'Thank you, I can see you're as efficient as ever,' he remarked coolly as he flicked through the details. Verity felt her pain being exchanged for anger at his taunting tone. She watched him with a dull fascination; she had only chosen the best locations, the most expensive of apartments, but he viewed them all quite uninterestedly. His eyes were barely looking at the attractive photographs of the buildings.

'Is none of them suitable?' she asked, suddenly anxious when there was no sign of approval. He raised his dark head swiftly, brushing his hair from his face as he did so. Their gazes met straight on, his cold ice-blue eyes penetrating deeply into her soft vivid blue ones. She returned his gaze with equal candour, mentally congratulating herself on her composure under his perceptive eyes.

'They're fine,' he said dismissively, passing them back to Verity.

'Thank you,' she replied abruptly.

He looked puzzled by her attitude for a moment, then said, 'Fax them to the Ellis home; Amanda is staying with her parents till things can be arranged.'

It was only natural that Amanda should stay there with her parents, but it brought memories flooding back for Verity. She gave a half-smile in response, and nodded.

It was unbearable; he seemed to be able to resume this businesslike manner with such apparent ease while her heart was being torn in two.

'There's nothing wrong, is there, Verity? Nothing I should know?' he asked.

'No, Mr Easton,' she replied efficiently. Nothing he should know, she stormed to herself as she left his office with as much dignity as she could muster. She went over to the fax machine, staring numbly at it, unable to think straight. How on earth was she to get through the day? she mused miserably. She began to prepare the brochures for sending, her mind in a vortex of emotion. She was so lost in her thoughts that she failed to notice that Saul had joined her.

'Verity,' he said softly, his warm breath caressing her ear. She jumped, the sudden proximity of his body making her breathing become erratic and her pulse increase. She turned to face him; he was too close, far too close. Verity retreated till her back pressed against the desk and she could move no further. Saul stood barely a foot away, his dark eyes darkening to a threatening ebony.

'Yes?' she stammered, sensing there was something wrong.

'The agency have just telephoned with regard to a replacement?' he queried.

Verity trembled and swallowed before replying. 'That's correct; I have been working my notice since I returned from France.'

'Why, Verity?' he asked, his face troubled.

Verity almost laughed aloud. *Why*? How could she answer him? she thought frantically, almost tempted to tell him the truth. How he had slowly eroded away every barrier she had erected to emotional involvement, only to leave her stranded and alone now that she was so vulnerable.

'I have decided to emigrate.'

'Emigrate?' he echoed in disbelief.

'Yes,' she continued, growing a little more confident, 'to Australia—all my family are over there,' she explained hurriedly.

'Australia?' he repeated almost angrily. 'You can't be serious!'

'Why not?' she flared. Did he honestly expect her to stay on here? The man was more insensitive than she thought; had she hidden her feelings with so much skill that he honestly had no idea?

'That's a bit extreme, isn't it?' his silky voice taunted.

'I think it's for the best—a new start for me and Hannah. My parents are longing for us to go,' she continued, hoping she sounded convincing.

'There's nothing to keep you here, then?' he asked dully, his eyes fixed on her, making her long to move away; but she was trapped. She tried to shrug her shoulders with feigned indifference, but he was too quick—with lightning speed he grabbed her. His facial expression alone was intimidating enough.

'You can't leave; what would I do without you?' he thundered, grabbing Verity by the shoulders as if to shake some sense into her.

She was frightened; why on earth was he behaving like this? She swallowed hard; her pulse was rapid and her heart was beating so fast that her chest hurt. 'I'm sure the agency will find a suitable replacement,' she countered, her eyes blazing as she tried to break loose from his grip.

'I don't want a suitable replacement, I want you!' he answered, still holding her, his face dark with fury.

'I have to go,' she pleaded, frightened that, if he did not release her soon, then the truth would come out.

'I can understand your not wanting to marry me, but I thought working together—I thought—well...' he paused while he thought '...I sort of hoped eventually...' His voice trailed away.

The silence that followed was filled with an electric tension. Verity was too frightened to speak in case it broke the magical spell. She stared at him in disbelief, her heart soaring, her mind a blank except for the words he had just said. It couldn't be true; was she hearing right? She faltered for a moment, unsure of what to say. Had she misheard him? She had longed, hoped, prayed for this moment for so long that she thought she was imagining it. She looked at him, her eyes wide with incredulity but brighter than they had been for days.

'You never asked me to marry you,' she said finally, her heart racing with anticipation. She began to pray, fast mental prayers to heaven. Let it be true, let him love me.

He stared at her for what seemed an eternity. 'Damn you, Verity, I did—twice!' He was almost yelling at her, but the love in his expression was evident. She was puzzled; he had asked her—asked her twice? Her mind was racing, trying to remember when this had all taken place. He knew she didn't understand, 'In France, the day after Amanda arrived, we talked about children needing two parents.' Realisation dawned and Verity gasped with surprise.

'I thought you meant you and Amanda!'

'That no doubt explains why you drank too much when we all went out to lunch!' He gave a deep, throaty laugh as he bent to kiss her, a long, lingering kiss that Verity willingly responded to. He kissed her tenderly, his hot lips on hers, then he began kissing slowly down from her neck towards the swollen peak of her breast, caressing it gently before sliding his strong hand to cup it. Then his hand went even lower, and she felt her body shudder at his touch. He wrapped his arm around her slim waist, squeezing her tightly.

'I have waited so long for you,' he muttered huskily. 'Why did I have to ask so many times? You don't know what you have put me through.'

Verity gasped in surprise, squirming away from his touch teasingly. 'What I've put *you* through?' she echoed incredulously. 'What about Amanda?' she demanded, but she smiled as she spoke, and remained close to him.

'Amanda? What has she got to do with it?' he asked, totally bewildered, wrapping his hand around her slim waist again to pull her close.

'I've been looking for properties for you two,' she retorted, longing to hear his explanation. Saul threw back his head and laughed, still holding her tightly as he did so, and Verity felt so blissfully happy and secure.

'It's true, Amanda has decided to return to England with a new lover, a much younger and richer man than Étienne.'

'Oh, I thought——' She gasped with pleasure as she realised the mistake she had made.

'I think we were both at cross purposes for so long that I was convinced you wouldn't marry me because of Jonathan,' Saul said, looking at her with such love that she felt the world spinning. She clung to him, raising her head so that he would kiss her. He lowered his head to hers and kissed her with such tenderness and longing that there was no mistaking how he felt. Verity felt dizzy with excitement, but she drew back, longing to know more.

'I stopped loving Jonathan long ago—perhaps even before Hannah was born—but I had been hurt. I didn't want to experience that again,' she confessed quietly.

'My darling, I know, I know,' he whispered gently, 'but you were so cool, so efficient and aloof that I thought it was hopeless.'

'How could you think that? Don't you remember France? I told you then—if not in words, certainly by my actions!' She coloured slightly as she recalled the events.

'How could I be sure? You went to France to see Étienne!' he reminded her with cold deliberation. Verity gave an involuntary shiver as she recalled what a fool she had made of herself.

'He was so persuasive, such a gentleman, sending me the roses then an air ticket . . .'

'I sent the roses,' he stated, waiting for her reaction.

'*You?*'

'Yes, I sent the first bouquet, but, as you seemed so convinced *he* had, who was I to argue?' he informed her, grinning widely.

'Why didn't you tell me, explain about it?' Verity asked, puzzled.

'Would you have believed me?' he asked. 'Étienne certainly had you fooled,' he reminded her grimly.

Verity flushed and snuggled closer to him. 'I'm sorry.'

'God, I was as mad as hell when you went to France!'

'I think I secretly did it to make you jealous,' she laughed.

'Well, lady, don't try anything like that again or you'll have the devil to pay. I'm a very jealous man!' he said, his voice quietly threatening as he drew her close, and squeezed her gently. Their arms entwined, their bodies became locked as one. The searing passion was mounting between them, demanding satisfaction, and the possibilty of work was rapidly fading.

'Let's finish for the day,' he whispered suggestively in her ear, and she smiled in agreement.

'I'll have to inform Reception we'll be out for the day,' she told him, and he threw back his head and laughed.

'Efficient as ever, Miss Chambers.'

Verity looked back up at him and smiled, knowing that soon she would be Mrs Easton...

Accept 4 Free Romances and 2 Free gifts

• F R O M   R E A D E R   S E R V I C E •

An irresistible invitation from Mills & Boon Reader Service. Please accept our offer of 4 free Romances, a CUDDLY TEDDY and a special MYSTERY GIFT... Then, if you choose, go on to enjoy 6 captivating Romances every month for just £1.60 each, postage and packing free. Plus our FREE newsletter with author news, competitions and much more.

Send the coupon below to:
Reader Service, FREEPOST, PO Box 236, Croydon, Surrey CR9 9EL.

NO STAMP REQUIRED

Yes! Please rush me my 4 Free Romances and 2 Free Gifts! Please also reserve me a Reader Service Subscription. If I decide to subscribe, I can look forward to receiving 6 new Romances every month for just £9.60, postage and packing is free. If I choose not to subscribe I shall write to you within 10 days - I can keep the books and gifts whatever I decide. I can cancel or suspend my subscription at any time. I am over 18 years of age.

Name Mrs/Miss/Ms/Mr _____ EP17R

Address _____

_____

Postcode _____ Signature _____

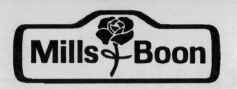

Next month's Romances

Each month, you can choose from a world of variety in romance with Mills & Boon. These are the new titles to look out for next month.

THE GOLDEN MASK ROBYN DONALD
THE PERFECT SOLUTION CATHERINE GEORGE
A DATE WITH DESTINY MIRANDA LEE
THE JILTED BRIDEGROOM CAROLE MORTIMER
SPIRIT OF LOVE EMMA GOLDRICK
LEFT IN TRUST KAY THORPE
UNCHAIN MY HEART STEPHANIE HOWARD
RELUCTANT HOSTAGE MARGARET MAYO
TWO-TIMING LOVE KATE PROCTOR
NATURALLY LOVING CATHERINE SPENCER
THE DEVIL YOU KNOW HELEN BROOKS
WHISPERING VINES ELIZABETH DUKE
DENIAL OF LOVE SHIRLEY KEMP
PASSING STRANGERS MARGARET CALLAGHAN
TAME A PROUD HEART JENETH MURREY

STARSIGN

GEMINI GIRL LIZA GOODMAN

Available from Boots, Martins, John Menzies, W.H. Smith, most supermarkets and other paperback stockists.

Also available from Mills & Boon Reader Service,
P.O. Box 236, Thornton Road, Croydon, Surrey CR9 3RU.